PRAISE FOR THE WATER WARS

"In the tradition of *The Hunger Games*, Cameron Stracher's *The Water Wars* is both a trenchant cautionary tale of a world drained of its most precious resource and a rousing adventure story of the plucky young heroes who set out to save it."

—Justin Cronin, author of *The Passage*

"*The Water Wars* is a gripping environmental thriller with a too-real message. Cameron Stracher tells a story with quick pacing, compelling characters, and a vision of a frightening future."

—Howard Gordon, executive producer of *24*
and author of *Gideon's War*

"Let us pray that the world which Cameron Stracher has invented in *The Water Wars* is testament solely to his pure, wild, and brilliant imagination, and not his ability to see the future. I was parched just reading it."

—Laurie David, Academy Award winning–producer of
An Inconvenient Truth and author of *The Down
to Earth Guide to Global Warming*

THE
WATER
WARS

THE
WATER
WARS

CAMERON STRACHER

Published by Sourcebooks Fire, an imprint of Sourcebooks, Inc.
P.O. Box 4410, Naperville, Illinois 60567-4410
(630) 961-3900
Fax: (630) 961-2168
teenfire.sourcebooks.com

Library of Congress Cataloging-in-Publication data is on file with the publisher.

Printed and bound in the United States of America.
SB 10 9 8 7 6 5 4 3 2 1

For Simon and Lulu

ARCTIC
ARCHEPELAGO

ISLAND OF
GREENLAND

EMPIRE OF CANADA

DAKOTAS

REPUBLIC OF
MINNESOTA

CALIFORNIA

ARIZONA

REPUBLIC OF
ILLINOWA

THE GREAT
COAST

REPUBLIC
OF TEXAS

REPUBLIC OF
LOUISIANA

NORTH AMERICA PRIOR
TO THE GREAT PANIC

NORTH AMERICA
POST-GREAT PANIC

CHAPTER 1

The year before he joined the Reclamation, when he was still seventeen, my brother Will set a new high score at the YouToo! booth at the gaming center. It was a record that stood for many years, and there were plenty of people who thought it would never be broken, although eventually it was. But by then my brother didn't care; he had found more important things to do than waste his time playing games in which winning only meant you had to play again.

We lived then in a time of drought and war. The great empires had fallen and been divided. The land was parched and starved for moisture, and the men who lived on it fought for every drop. Outside, the wind howled like something wounded. Inside, our skin flaked, and our eyes stung and burned. Our tongues were like thick snakes asleep in dark graves.

That's why I'll never forget the first time I saw Kai. He was standing in the open road drinking a glass of water like it didn't matter—water from an old plastene cup. There could have been anything in that cup: bacteria or a virus or any of the other poisons they taught about at school. Men had dug so deep for water that salt had leached into the wells, and unnamed diseases lived in what remained. But Kai didn't seem to care. He drank his water like it was the simplest thing in the world. I knew it was water because when he was finished, he did something extraordinary: he flipped the cup upside down and spilled the last remaining drops into the dust.

"Hey!" I called out to him. "You can't do that!"

He looked at me like he didn't know I was the only other person on the deserted road. He was about the same age as Will. Both had that lanky boy body I had just begun to recognize: hip bones and wrists, flat bellies and torsos. But while Will and I were dark-haired and lean, Kai was blond, with skin that glowed in the morning sun. I felt an urge to run my fingertips over his smooth forearms, feel the strange softness against my ragged nails that I never let grow long enough to paint like other girls did.

"Who says I can't?" he asked.

Wasting water was illegal. There were fines, and even prison sentences, for exceeding the quotas. But this boy looked like he didn't care about any of that.

"You just can't," I said.

"That's something a shaker would say."

"Because it's true."

"How do you know?"

"I know—that's all. Look around. Do you see any water here?"

"There's plenty of water," said the boy.

"Yeah, in the ocean."

"Can't drink salt water," he said, as if I didn't know.

I looked down the dusty road. Not a sign of life anywhere—just the hills, scarred from ancient fires, and sand blowing around the empty lot where I waited. Not even a lizard or an insect moved.

Once there had been a row of stores at the edge of the lot, but now all that remained were the skeletons that scavengers hadn't sold for scrap. Torn insulation and loose wire dangled like innards from pitted aluminum struts. When the wind blew, they made a sound like mourning.

"Why don't you have your screen, anyway?" A new student should at least bring a notebook to his first day, I thought.

"I don't go to school."

"Are you a harvester?"

"My father says I don't have to go to school."

Everyone went to school, except for water harvesters' kids who chased the clouds across the sky. At least until you were eighteen— then you got jobs, or joined the army, or worked for the Water Authority Board, which was like staying in school for life.

"You're lucky," I said.

"School's not so bad."

I liked school, although I wouldn't admit it. I loved learning the details about shiny rocks, their hard, encrusted surfaces yielding clues about the minerals inside. I loved our field trips to the dams, where metal wheels as large as entire houses turned slowly in their silicon beds. Best of all, I loved deciphering the swirling purple patterns of thunderstorms and hurricanes, trying to predict where, on the brown-gray prairie, they would strike next.

"Did they take you out?" I asked.

He shrugged. "Didn't need to go anymore."

I peered down the road again. The bus was late. It was often late. Sometimes it didn't come at all, and I had to walk back to my building, where my father would unplug the old car and drive me to the school in town. Will was already there, a full hour earlier, because he had to empty the basins before the sun evaporated the small amount of water that collected as dew. Last year two other girls rode the bus with me, but one day they stopped coming and never returned. It was boring waiting alone. I welcomed the distraction.

"I've got a brother," I said. "He passed his army physical."

"Easy."

"He had to do fifty pushups."

"I can do a hundred."

The boy kneeled like he was going to start exercising right there in the dust. The place where he had spilled his cup was completely dry; I couldn't even tell it had been wet. I could see the elastic band of his underwear and the smooth skin where his back was exposed. No marks, scratches, or scabs of any kind. My own hands looked like some kind of treasure map, except the lines didn't lead to riches.

"I'm Vera," I said to his back.

"Kai," he said, standing up.

"Where did you get the water?"

"I've got lots of water."

"Are you rich?"

"I guess so."

"Should you be out alone?"

"Ha!" he snorted. "I'd like to see them try something."

It wasn't clear whom he was talking about, but I didn't think

Kai—or any boy—could stand up well to the bandits and soldiers who menaced our town, no matter how many pushups he could do.

"Are you waiting for someone?" I asked.

"Going to a scavenge site. Want to come?"

"I've got school."

"After school?"

I said I would try, but I knew my father wouldn't let me. He didn't want me going anywhere after school—not with this boy, not with any boy. It was dangerous to hang around strangers. Just last year there had been a virus, and three kids in our class had died. No one went to school for two weeks afterward, and Will and I played cards in his bedroom until we got so bored that we wanted to scream.

"We live in the Wellington Pavilion," Kai said, naming a fancy housing complex. "Meet me there this afternoon. I'll tell the guards."

"I have water team."

"After water team, then."

"I'll ask my dad." Down the road I could see the telltale signs of rising dust. "There's my bus."

Kai looked to where I pointed, and his lips drew a tight line of disappointment. I realized then that he wasn't out in the road spilling water because he had enough to drink. Like the girls who cut themselves or snuck their parents' pharmies, he wanted someone to pay attention. I promised myself I would try to visit this boy, even though my father wouldn't like it.

"Good-bye," I said. "I'll look for you later."

"Later," he said.

I boarded the bus and turned to wave, but as I did, I saw a car stop for the boy—a big, black limousine, gasoline-powered, with an engine that threw off heat in shimmering waves of silver. The door opened, and a burly guard with a machine pistol stepped into the road—mirrored glasses hid his eyes, and a thick cartridge belt cinched his waist. He signaled to Kai, and the boy climbed inside without looking back.

CHAPTER 2

That night Will and I stayed up late. Will had dragged his mattress across the hallway to my room, where it rested on a couple of wooden crates our father had salvaged from a food drop. The two beds made a kind of giant spongy stair. I was on the top step, and Will was one below. We had two covers, both of which I tugged more closely around me. Will complained, but he gave up as soon as I told him about Kai.

"He must be rich," Will concluded.

"He is," I said. "And Will…" I waited until I had his complete attention. "After the bus came, they picked him up in a limo."

"Who picked him up?"

"I don't know. There was a guard with a gun."

Will squinted with his left eye. I always thought it was unfair that I got our mother's freckles, while Will had our father's witch-hazel eyes: pinwheels of green, gray, and gold. When he squinted, it was like peering into the glass end of a kaleidoscope.

"His father must be a WAB minister, maybe."

"There are no WABs here," I reminded him.

"He could live in Basin."

"Then why would he be out walking on our road?" I asked.

If the boy's father were on the Water Authority Board, he wouldn't live in the Wellington Pavilion, as nice as it was, and he wouldn't be outside walking. There were places a lot nicer, and a lot more expensive, with better security. Most of the WAB ministers lived in Basin, the capitol, about sixty kilometers away. The Water Authority controlled the flow and distribution of water and was the closest thing we had to an actual government. Our republic—Illinowa—was all that remained of the Midwestern pieces of the old United States, and the only thing left to govern was water. The decisions made by WABs in Basin could mean life or death for the rest of us. I'd never been to the city, but photographs showed leafy trees growing from beneath semi-porous grates and real grass in the park. Everything seemed to be breathing, and the air was gauzy with moisture.

"He must live around here," I decided. "He says he does."

"We should invite him to dinner."

"We don't have any food."

"That's not true."

"Synth-food's not food," said Will. "And Dad is a terrible cook."

"He doesn't have time to make a real meal." I hated when Will criticized our father's cooking. "Anyway, I don't mind synth-steaks."

It was months since we'd eaten anything except the synthetic food the Water Authority Board provided in weekly food drops. They claimed it tasted like the real thing, but of course it didn't. Everything had a sort of bland sameness. Steak tasted like chicken; orange juice tasted like tomato juice. The only real differences were the colors and textures. Still, people could get used to anything, and we did.

If Kai was rich, he didn't act like it. Rich people lived in secure compounds with guards and robo-dogs and rarely left their buildings. When they did, they wore kev-jackets on the streets and carried laser-tasers or guns. In Basin they were permitted to shoot first if a stranger approached without identification. Even in Arch, where we lived, the occasional businessman was ferried about in an armored vehicle. You could never be too safe, or too protected. That's what our teachers said. Men would kill for a glass of water, and did.

Will and I talked until the power grid shut down and the lights flickered, then went dark. He had a small glow light, but it wasn't fully charged or bright enough for both of us to read by. The darkness settled. I felt myself growing weightless, thoughts flitting half-formed through my mind, pieces of one thing replaced by endings of another. I knew sleep was coming. In my dreams Kai offered me plastene cups filled with water, but I couldn't drink them fast enough. The water tasted like graphite and made my mouth dry. I tried to tell him to stop, but he kept offering them and spilling what I couldn't drink on the ground.

When I awoke, my blanket was bunched around my neck, and my hair was damp with sweat. Will was already downstairs, dry-showered and eating a bowl of Oatios in front of the wireless. I skipped the shower and grabbed a Toasty Bar as our father ushered us to the door.

"No time for texting," he said.

I reached for a controller on the kitchen table.

"Signal's out anyway," said Will.

9

The wireless played a news feed about a pirate attack, and Will also had a couple of game channels open, but the wi-text screen was down. My father had explained that bandwidth and signal strength varied depending on the grid, but it didn't seem a coincidence that propaganda and entertainment were always easiest to find while communication was more difficult. You could play YouToo! almost anywhere in the world, but sending a simple message across republics was unpredictable and sometimes impossible.

I hurried to follow Will and barely had time to finish my breakfast because he walked so fast.

We didn't see Kai at the bus stop. We waited until the last possible minute, staring down the road in the hope that he would materialize out of the dust. Then the driver barked for us to get on board, and we scampered up the steps. The ride to school was agonizingly slow and bumpy. Though it was fall, it felt like summer, and the bus was hot and airless even with the windows cranked open. My lips were chapped, and I was thirsty already, but of course there was nothing to drink and there wouldn't be anything until lunchtime. I licked my lips and plunged into the pages of my screen, where the seas were always blue and the skies heavy with thunder.

Our school was a one-story cinder-block building that looked as if it had once been larger. At each end the hallways simply stopped and were bricked off without windows or doors. The classrooms were overcrowded, and there wasn't enough space in the gym or lunchroom for everyone to play or eat at the same time. Fortunately on most days one-quarter of the kids were sick or absent, which meant the school was nearly the right size for the rest of us. At least there were enough chairs in my class for everyone to find a seat.

The school's venti-unit blew at full power. I could feel the air coursing over my head like a current as I walked down the hallway. It was crackly and dry, alive with static electricity. The unit was supposed to filter dirt and chemicals, but it made the air taste like something metallic. The teachers kept the windows open anyway, because the school was so hot.

I found my class and sat at my usual seat near the window. The other kids chatted noisily and tossed things at each other while I opened my screen and adjusted my pen-writer. A boy named Ryark tried to get my attention by tapping my shoulder with a calculating stick. He had hair that stuck up like a toilet brush. I ignored him. When the teacher arrived, Ryark sat back quickly in his seat, and the class quieted down. No one dared aggravate the teachers, who freely dispensed electric zaps with a battery-powered teacher's aid.

We were doing a unit on weather. Mrs. Delfina used her laser pencil to show how the jet stream carried storm systems from west to east. Variations in Earth's temperature made the jet stream dip and twist, curving north when it should be headed east. This made it snow where it should be warm and brought rain to the colder regions. Predicting weather, she said, was more art than science, because you had to take into account the changing temperature of the land and water and the competing forces of high and low pressure systems that jockeyed for position over the continent. Even the slightest variation could wreak enormous havoc.

"A butterfly beating its wings over Basin today," Mrs. D. said, "can change tomorrow's weather two thousand kilometers away."

I pictured a butterfly floating in the jet stream—beating its wings furiously to stay aloft—and moving just enough air so storm clouds would travel north instead of south. It was difficult to imagine, although I knew men changed the weather with giant airplanes that seeded the clouds for rain and enormous turbines that sucked the moisture from the sky. Many days we awoke with storm clouds on the horizon, only to see the sky transformed into a brilliant, piercing blue.

"What's the most important thing we can do to protect our weather?" Mrs. D. asked.

"Guard the earth and sky," we answered in unison.

Mrs. Delfina smiled. Her teeth were large and white and looked nearly perfect. In fact, I knew they were not real. I had seen her once, in the bathroom, with her teeth on the side of the sink, her open mouth hollow and empty. Teeth were the first thing that went bad, and most shakers had to make do with fake ones. Mrs. D. was lucky she could afford them. There were plenty who could not.

When we finished morning lessons, there was lunch, which we ate in the cafeteria. The school had stopped providing hot lunch several years ago. Now most kids brought lunch from home. I traded my Cheesios to another girl for an extra soy milk. Nearby a group of boys tossed packs of dried veggies at each other. I looked around for Will, but I didn't see him. I drank the first milk, and then the second, and still I was thirsty. But there would be no more until dinner, so I forced my lips shut and tried to think about something else.

During recess some of the younger kids went outside, even though the school forbade it. There weren't enough teachers to prevent them, and they snuck out through the cafeteria doors. I sat near a window with my screen and watched them kick a small ball around in the dust. When they came back inside, they were sweaty and dirty and laughing. One boy started coughing, and the others made fun of him, holding their hands over their mouths and whooping. The first boy looked as if he might start crying, and I nearly stood up to tell the others to stop. But then the bell rang; school resumed, and the rest of the day passed quickly. More lessons in weather, then water management and conservation, then math.

After school I stayed late for water team. I got to work with the seniors, because I was tall for my age, and our supervisor thought I was older. I helped one girl clear the drains where the morning dew trickled into the catch basins. We found a dead snake, which made the girl shriek. I lifted it by its tail and tossed it into the garbage. Dead things never bothered me. Once they were dead, I figured, they couldn't harm anyone.

Afterward I waited for Will. He was leader of a team working with the condensers on the roof. It was tricky climbing the pitted walls where the ladders had cracked and split, but Will was nimble and quick and found footholds when others could not. I saw him walking from the traps near the recycling barrels with his head high and several other children following him. He pretended not to notice, but I could tell that he was proud to be in charge.

We didn't talk much on the ride back home. School was exhausting even though very little got done. Will's shoulders drooped and his head lolled toward the window as if he couldn't hold it up. As for me, I felt like there was cotton in my head. Although the ride was noisy and bumpy, we both fell asleep somewhere before home.

The driver woke us at our stop. We staggered from the bus and trudged along the sandy path to our building. There was no shade, and the sun on our heads was like a dull, throbbing drum. Our building was nearly a kilometer from the main road, and the walk left us coated in a gray, sooty dust. When we arrived at the entrance, Will punched in the code for the security gate, and I pushed it open.

Our father was waiting for us by the front door to our apartment. It was always a surprise to see how much he had aged in the last year. The lines around his eyes and mouth had deepened, and his cheeks sunk where once they stretched. He was always slim, but he seemed thinner—almost gaunt. His black hair was now flecked with gray, and the hazel in his eyes was closer to brown than green. I kissed him hello, and he smiled slightly.

"Hi, Daddy," I said.

"How was school?" he asked.

I made up a story about being asked to lead the class in a prayer, and this made him happy. Although not religious, he liked to tell us there was some higher purpose to life that would eventually be revealed. This was something he had started talking about only in the last year—only since our mother had gotten sick.

"Are you hungry?" he asked.

I said I wasn't, although I hadn't eaten since before noon. Will just ignored him and headed for the back bedroom. I looked at my father and shrugged, then followed Will.

Since the headaches had crippled her, our mother spent nearly every day in her room, emerging only to use the bathroom. It was impossible for her to rise in the morning or to tolerate sunlight. All the shades were drawn and the lights turned low. There was something in the air that smelled like mint, and the ventilation system that cycled it made the room sweet and pungent. It was part of the medicine the doctors prescribed, but I suspected it was nothing more than perfume. Medicine was expensive and in short supply, and most doctors were fakes anyway.

Our mother seemed shrunken on the bed, the pillows like giant beanbags behind her. Her eyes were closed, and I could barely see the rest of her face above the big blanket that covered her body. Our father stepped into the room behind Will. He appeared to be waiting for someone to speak, but Will just stood quietly as if he were weighing something.

I couldn't bear the silence. "Hi, Mom," I said. "We just got home from school."

Our mother opened her eyes. "Hello, Vera." Her voice sounded as if it had emerged from a great depth.

"Are you feeling okay?"

"The light. It hurts my eyes."

"Should I shut it off?" Our mother waved weakly, which could have been yes or no.

"It's not the light," said Will. "It's the water."

"There's nothing wrong with the water," said our father.

"She needs fresh water," said Will. He was moving quickly now toward her table, grabbing the bottles of various sizes beside her, trying to hold them all in his hands, knocking them against each other.

"Will, please," said our mother.

"You have to drink some clean water!"

"You'll break them!" warned our father.

But Will emptied the bottles as if they were filled with poison, spraying liquid through the air. His hands flailed above his head as he emptied their contents in a frenzy of fury and frustration. One bottle slipped from his hand and shattered on the floor, pink liquid oozing between shards of glass. He looked as if he might smash another and raised his arms to throw it.

Our father grabbed him and pulled him down, but Will continued to struggle. Although our father was heavier, he was a few centimeters shorter than Will, and I worried Will would hurt him.

"Stop it! Stop it!" I cried.

"Will?" our mother asked.

But Will couldn't answer. He was sobbing on the floor.

CHAPTER 3

Maybe it was the water. Maybe it was the air. Maybe it was the earth itself. Whatever the cause, people were sick, and not just our mother. In our building, eight adults had been to the hospital in the last month alone. Most of them were not old, and two were young enough to still live with their parents. At school kids were always absent with colds or coughs, and even I had a sore throat for most of the winter. Will complained of aches in his muscles, which our father treated with warm compresses and synaspirin. It seemed like there was always an ambulette parked in front of our building or racing down the street.

The teachers taught us to cover our mouths when we coughed and to wash our hands. Germs were spread by contact, they said, and children were always touching things. But Will said germs were in the air, carried by the wind. We couldn't help breathing them, eating them. That's supposedly why the school had venti-units. But the units actually made things worse, because they trapped germs and blew them around. Shakers thought they were cleaning the air, but really they were dirtying it.

"They're making us sick," Will insisted.

We were in the back of the old electric car, driving with our father to the water distribution center. The car whined and lurched on the potholed road. Our father had forgotten to plug it in before the power grid switched off the previous night, and the battery was nearly drained.

"It doesn't work that way," said our father. "No one can make you sick."

"If someone sneezes on you, they can make you sick," I said.

"This is different," our father said. "Will blames the Water Authority for making your mother sick."

"Did they?" I asked.

"Of course not!"

"How do you know?" Will demanded.

The car stalled and stopped. Our father muttered a curse under his breath. He thought we couldn't hear him. He placed both hands on the wheel and turned around to face us.

"First of all, the Water Authority is not a person," he explained. "If they made anyone sick, there would be reports about it—news texts, public hearings. People would notice."

"Will noticed," I pointed out.

"Second," said our father, ignoring me, "the Water Authority takes care of us. They don't make us sick."

"Maybe it was an accident."

Our father sighed. "I know this is hard for you. It's hard for all of us. But your mother is getting good medicine, and the doctors say she can get better. She just needs rest."

"She won't get better," said Will.

"Will!" I said.

"She won't, Vera. She's sick. As long as she keeps drinking their water, she's going to stay sick."

"So what should she do? Stop drinking?"

"We should take her someplace where the water is clean."

"Basin?"

"Basin's no better."

"What about us? Shouldn't we stop drinking the water?"

Will nodded. "We'll get sick too before long."

"Stop that talk!" said our father, interrupting us. "We're not going anywhere. This is our home." The car suddenly lurched forward, throwing us against our seats. "Now I want you to quit it, Will," our father said. "Your mother is going to get better. She will."

Normally Will wouldn't quiet down so easily. Even if he was wrong, he spoke with such conviction that it seemed he must be right. In those days, when we argued, I usually gave in before he did. Everyone did. He had the kind of intensity that made adults look to him as a leader and had kids currying his favor.

But Will didn't respond, and our father drove the rest of the way in silence.

When we arrived at the center, I grabbed a free cart while our father and Will unloaded the empty bottles. The center was crowded with other families picking up their weekly supply, and we stopped to chat with people we knew. The Jarviks lived in our apartment complex, and their son Tyler was in Will's class. Tyler was a skinny boy with acne who coughed frequently and picked at the scabs on his face. Will didn't like him, but he pretended to, just to be polite. I felt sorry for Tyler, because he never had enough to drink at lunchtime and was always begging other kids to trade him water or syn-juice for the hard soy crackers his mother packed in his lunch box. But the crackers were stale and crumbly, and he rarely found a taker.

A man was selling coupons from a ration book, and I suggested we buy a pack. Our father said we had enough water for the week and didn't need any more coupons. This wasn't exactly true. We weren't as thirsty as Tyler, but we never had enough water either. For weeks the only work my father had was part-time—repairing hoses for a small business that did a decent trade in used rubber parts. He made barely enough money to pay for a nurse to check in on my mother. But I didn't want to disagree with him—not after his disagreement with Will—and I knew he really meant we couldn't *afford* more water. Everyone wanted more water; they just couldn't pay for it.

There was plenty of water for sale at the driller's market downtown; but here, in the distribution center, the only water was rationed, government-issued, in familiar blue and white bottles. It wasn't "real" water, Will explained, but desalinated water. This meant it came from the ocean and was processed in a giant factory where all the minerals were removed and chemicals added so it was fit for drinking. The bottles didn't disclose their origin, but you could tell the water was desalinated because it felt slippery on the tongue and had a tangy aftertaste—like licking a burnt match. After a long, dry summer, the Water Authority imported extra bottles of seawater in trade with the Great Coast for building materials like limestone and granite.

We waited in line behind a family of seven whose cart was stacked high with bottles. Our father had only four coupons, so we purchased only two bottles. I was already thirsty and planning how I could fill my canteen from the fountain at school when the monitors weren't watching. In a pinch I could drink tap water, but that could really make a person sick. The hospitals wouldn't even treat a patient who drank tap water; they claimed it was a "self-inflicted" injury. It had happened to one of our neighbors, and he lost forty pounds and never fully recovered. If our mother was being poisoned, we were all being poisoned. We had to drink *something*. A person could go without food for a month, but dehydration could kill within days. This was why we bought water at the distribution center rather than on the black market or even from the drillers. It was the least likely to kill us.

After buying water our father took us to buy some new clothes. He complained we grew so fast that nothing fit for longer than six months. Will went through shoes like rags. I tore holes in the knees of my pants. Although our father exaggerated, it wasn't far from the truth. It took two chemo washes to remove the dirt from my jeans, and even Will's best shoes had holes in the soles.

I loved shopping. When my mother was well, we would spend hours going through the racks, fingering the dresses and blouses she loved to wear. Her favorite color was green, which she said redheads weren't supposed to wear, but I always thought the clothes she picked looked beautiful on her. She would throw together an old top with a forgotten skirt, and suddenly she looked as if she had spent the whole day getting ready. It was a skill I couldn't copy, hard as I tried. The same clothes that looked glamorous with her red hair looked drab with my dark brown bangs, and my small nose made everything I wore seem too childlike.

I needed new jeans, but I also needed tops and a new pair of shoes. My shirts were too short, and my toes were scrunched. But I didn't say anything to my father, because I saw the way he looked when he fingered the price tags on the outfits I handed him. "Do you really need three?" he asked. I shook my head and pulled my favorite from the bunch—a floral print top with green swirling patterns that reminded me of clouds. It was made from a synthetic fiber called *cattan* that felt slightly oily to the touch. "This one," I said. I told myself that one outfit was better than none. As for the shoes, I would just have to keep squeezing my feet into the ones I had.

Will picked a new pair of jeans. Our father took Will's pants and my top to the cash register where he paid with his credit chip.

Then it was back to the car for our last stop of the day: the grocery store.

Our father could cook almost anything with nothing. Even when our mother was well, our father did most of the cooking. Now as we roamed the aisles, he fingered the synth-fruit and quasi-vocados, checking for ripeness and disease. "How do you feel about guacamole?" he asked.

We felt great about guacamole—which gave me an idea.

"Kai loves Mexican food," I said, though I had no clue if this were true.

"Kai? The boy in the limousine?" our father asked.

"He's lonely."

"His parents would never let him visit for dinner."

"We could text them our certificates."

"Even so, he doesn't need fake food."

"He might want a home-cooked meal," Will piped up, coming to my aid.

Our father considered this. None of us could remember the last time we had guests at our apartment. The three of us ate quickly at our small table, often in silence, the gloom of illness like a shroud. Loneliness was something we understood, even in a crowd.

Soon we were grabbing the ingredients for a Mexican feast off the half-empty shelves at the store: a package of synth-tortillas, another package of chips, a bottle of salsa made with three percent real tomatoes, and a bag of soy cheese. Our father even bought a six-pack of Beer-o, which he claimed was almost as good as the real thing, although Will made a face behind his back like he was gagging. I pushed the cart while our father inspected items on the shelves, reading their ingredients and hefting them in his hands as if he could discern the harmful chemicals simply by weighing them.

This was our happy father, the one I remembered from the days when our mother would take us shopping, singing songs about *to-may-toes* and *to-mah-toes* that always made us laugh. Our mother had been the silly one, but since she had become sick, there was very little silliness in our house.

"It's a lot of food for four, and even more for three," said our father. "Let's hope he can make it."

In the parking lot, the car started right away, and our father let Will drive home. He leaned into the steering wheel, grasping it with both hands, while our father kept one hand close to the emergency brake. The sun was low in the sky, and for once it looked warm rather than desolate. Even the fake flowers in the window boxes outside our building looked brighter, as if they had bloomed in our absence. We coasted onto the entrance road, and Will executed a perfect turn into the garage.

While our father mashed quasi-vocados in the kitchen and Will rehydrated the beans, I tried to reach Kai on the wireless using the ID he had given me. But after fifteen minutes without a signal, I gave up in frustration.

Kai lived only three kilometers from our building—a quick ride in the car or on my pedicycle—but at first my father didn't want to hear about it.

"At this hour who knows who's on the road?" he said.

"I'll text you as soon as I get there."

"You just said the wireless isn't working."

"It probably works at Kai's."

We went back and forth for a while, but eventually my father gave in, as I knew he would. I could tell he was excited about a visitor—especially someone wealthy and mysterious—and now that he was making all this food, someone had to eat it.

Our family lived in a section of Arch called "the Rails" where trains had once rumbled. Long ago it had been one of the least expensive places to live, but after the transportation system broke down, it was one of the few places where food and water were still available. As the other suburbs collapsed, the Rails survived and even thrived. But the legacy of poverty was hard to shake, and anything that reminded us of plenty held us in an incantatory grip.

It was an easy ride to the Wellington Pavilion. No one passed me on the road, and the wind at my back made pedaling easier. The guards stopped me by the front gate, and I removed my goggles to show them copies of my Certification of Health and Vaccination. Still, they wouldn't let me inside. Instead they called Kai on an intercom, and in a few minutes he appeared.

"Hi," I said. "Are you hungry?"

When he cocked his head, he looked like a sunflower, I thought, a rare prize that grew only in hothouses: tall, reedy, with silky blond hair that shone in the twilight. "What are you doing here?" he asked.

"Inviting you to dinner."

"When?"

"Now." I held out copies of our certifications, and he took them tentatively in his hand.

"What are you cooking?"

"It's a surprise."

He was only gone for five minutes. When he returned, he carried two plastene jugs and a small satchel on his hip. The jugs were stamped with a seal from the Water Authority, certifying that they contained real water from pure aquifers. He beckoned to me, and the guards stood by indifferently as I entered the compound. In a moment the black limousine appeared from an underground driveway, its powerful gasoline engine growling hungrily. It circled the interior courtyard and stopped in front of Kai. The bodyguard stepped from the driver's side, machine pistol at the ready, mirrored glasses on the bridge of his nose.

"Come on," Kai said to me. "We'll drive you."

"I have my cycle."

"Martin will bring it back after he drops us off."

I looked at the bodyguard, but his eyes were impassive behind the lenses. He stood there, alert, one hand holding open the door, the other on that machine pistol, head constantly scanning for threats.

I climbed into the car and folded myself into the back seat. It smelled richly of leather and coconut—scents I knew only from chemo-washes. There was a glass divider between the front and back, and below the divider—incredibly—were a sink, a dozen small bottles of colored liquid, and six plastene liter bottles of water.

"It's a bar," said Kai when he noticed me staring.

"What's it do?"

"It doesn't *do* anything." He smiled at my ignorance. "You mix drinks for yourself."

Of course I knew what alcohol was, but no one I knew mixed it with anything. At parties sometimes shakers would pass around home-brewed stuff, and I had even seen my father take a glass every now and then, but no one had the money to mix real alcohol with other liquids. When I looked at Kai I had to remind myself to stop staring at his skin. It wasn't calloused or dry like paper. A faint scent—real soap, I realized—emanated from his hair. It was all I could do to stop myself from touching him, and I felt my face grow hot from the thought.

The ride was luxurious and smooth. I'd never been in a car like this. The limo's big tires absorbed every jolt in the road, and its thick windows and doors (bulletproof, Kai said) blocked outside noise. We barely had time for a few words of conversation before we arrived at the front entrance of our building. Martin parked near the unmanned gate, then came around to unlock our doors. Kai gave him instructions for dropping off my cycle, and the man nodded wordlessly. He waited—gun at the ready—while we walked upstairs. My father opened the door. He was wiping his hands on his thighs, but when he saw the water, he stopped.

"Thank you for having me to dinner," said Kai.

"You didn't have to do that."

"Dad." I scolded. "This is Kai."

"I'm sorry. Where are my manners?" He accepted the jugs. "Thank you, Kai," he added. "It's nice to meet you." His voice sounded hoarse.

Will appeared at his side, and his gaze went right to the water jugs. Without a word he took one bottle from our father's hand and retreated to the back bedroom. Before Kai could ask any questions, I ushered him into the living room, where my father's guacamole awaited. It was delicious, as always—the perfect blend of tangy salsa and creamy quasi-vocados. We had scooped up half the bowl when Will returned. His eyes were red-rimmed, but he was wearing a broad smile. "She drank a little," he said.

"This is Kai." It had been rude of Will to leave without even so much as a nod, but if he noticed my sarcasm, he pretended to ignore it. He said hello, then spooned himself some guacamole. Soon the boys were sitting on the couch chatting about the latest

YouToo! and We! uploads. I followed their conversation like it was a Ping match: from screen to screen to screen. They could have been brothers of different mothers: one blond and smooth, the other ragged and lean, both tapered and fine.

Our father returned from the kitchen. Kai looked at his empty plate longingly. "I've never had guacamole," he said.

"It's my dad's specialty," I told him.

"My dad can't cook," Kai said.

"I haven't met your parents," said our father. "Are they registered?" Adults who had passed a rigorous security screening were allowed to travel freely between the lower republics and often had diplomatic or important business jobs.

"My father's a driller."

This wasn't the answer anyone expected, but it made perfect sense. Drillers were wildcatters, risk-takers, and often rich—if they found water. That explained the limousine and the bodyguard.

"Why aren't you in school?" our father asked.

"My dad needs me. He says I don't have to go."

"What about your mother?"

"She died when I was a baby."

We were silent for a moment, remembering. Before our mother had gotten sick, there was little she hadn't done: school activities, recycling duties, and lots of volunteer projects. She had been the water-smart mom in my class all through elementary school. For Will's prom, she taught the boys how to dance. When I remembered those times, I saw our mother in a favorite green hat, her red hair corkscrewing to her shoulders. People said I resembled her, but it was only the freckles. I wished I were as pretty as my mother. Every time I looked at my own arms, my hands, and my legs, the freckles seemed to mock my pale skin and uninteresting mouth—not at all like our mother's vibrant lips and high cheekbones. Who would want to kiss such boring lips or such a flat pale brow? I knew it was petty to think those things, but thinking about anything else only made me sadder.

"Why don't we head to the kitchen?" said our father. "Dinner's ready."

He had set the table with the "good" china—plates that required sanitizing before putting them away—as well as silverware, glasses, and even smaller plates for the chips and salsa. Four fat candles glowed, spilling light onto our mother's favorite tablecloth: silver threads in a rich red fabric. Three bowls of various sizes bubbled and steamed. The food itself was like a decoration, the brightly colored peppers contrasting with the browns of the beans and the tans of the tortillas. Everything looked perfect.

Before he sat down Kai withdrew something that looked like a thick laser pencil from his satchel. He lifted his shirt and jabbed at the fleshy side of his stomach. Then he took his place at the table and smoothed his napkin over his lap as if nothing had happened. We couldn't help but stare.

"It's for the sugar before I eat," he explained.

"You have diabetes," said our father.

"Yes. Since I was thirteen."

Diabetes was an old-fashioned disease, one I had heard about but never seen. The bodies of people with diabetes didn't produce insulin. Without it, diabetics could die within weeks. Kai had his insulin tucked inside a pencil: real medication that must have cost a fortune—and that kept him alive.

Despite his wealth, however, Kai ate as if he were famished. He piled his plate, then had second helpings—and thirds. Even Will couldn't keep up. Our father poured from Kai's jugs, and we each drank two glasses of water. I couldn't believe how good it tasted: crisp and pure, almost like nothing at all. There was no bad aftertaste, no lingering hint of salt or algae. I held the glass aloft, and the water sparkled gold, green, and silver in the light.

"It's delicious," I said.

"We drilled it from an upper-republic aquifer," said Kai.

"I thought we had drained all our aquifers," said Will.

"Not all of them. There are still some left—if you know where to look. You have to get beneath the surface."

"How do you know where to look?"

"My father knows."

Of course no driller would share his secrets. There were plenty of tales about how drillers found water—divining rods and specially trained animals, sunspots and moonbeams. But if any of these methods worked, there were no screens verifying it and no witnesses except the driller himself and his closest confidantes. Water was money, and money was power, and no one would give up one without the promise of the other.

"Once there was water flowing down in rivers from the mountains into the sea," said our father.

"They were thousands of kilometers long," added Kai. "During the rains they would flood and wash everything away."

"Yes. You could drink it and bathe in it. People even used the rivers to clean their clothes."

When the teachers taught about that time, they made it seem as if the rivers were viewed as inconvenient and expensive highways, wasted resources pouring out into the ocean. Now dams caught all the water, powered turbines, and irrigated the land. Water was too valuable to let it flood the prairies and spill into the sea.

"Your mother and I sailed on a river once," said our father. "It was thick, fast, and, in some places, hundreds of meters deep."

"When was that?" I asked.

"Before you were born. In Sahara, when it was known as Africa."

I had never heard this story before, but I knew my father didn't like to talk about the earlier times: the world before the wars and water shortages. When he was a boy, there were still green fields and blue lakes. Kids played sports outside, like baseball and football, that existed now only on the screens. You could lie in a tub filled with warm water for no reason except to relax. It seemed foolish and wasteful and wonderful—to live as if the sky were endless and time itself had no measure.

"Do you think we'll ever be able to travel down a river again?" I asked.

"No." Our father shook his head sadly. "But long after people are gone, the rivers will return."

I had never heard our father talking like this, and I wondered if Kai's presence had loosened his tongue.

Then Kai spoke. "I know a river."

"Where?" I asked.

"I can't say."

"Can you sail down it?"

Kai ignored my question. "My father told me."

"Tell us," said Will. "We can keep a secret."

"I promised my father."

"If your father knows a river," said our father, "he should tell the government."

Kai laughed. He didn't sound like a kid at all. His laugh was scratchy and untidy, like an adult cackling at a dirty joke. To tell the truth, it scared me a little. "The government is stupid," he said.

This was scandalous. Even Will seemed shocked. No one said that about the government. It could get a person—even a teenager—arrested.

"Kai," our father said gently. "We don't say those kinds of things."

"Why not, if they're true?"

Our father sighed and looked down at his hands. Then he looked up and said, "These are difficult times, Kai. It's not like when I was growing up. We have to watch what we eat and drink and be careful of what we say. The world is a dangerous place, and the government is just trying to protect us. There are bad people out there who want to do bad things. Sometimes, to protect all of us, some of us can't say everything we want to say."

"It's about the water, isn't it, Dad?" asked Will.

"It started with the water," said our father. "But now it's about so many different things."

Will squinted, his left eye nearly closed, the green in his iris like a sliver of emerald. I knew he was thinking about the war, and the army, and what awaited him next year. I was too. Everyone spent a year in the military, then five years afterward on active reserve. We had to protect Illinowa—guard the earth and sky. But the Rails seemed a long way from Basin, and I wondered who was really protecting whom.

A klaxon rang outside signaling the last hour before the grid shut down. I could hear the car outside waiting, the low humming of its motor like the grid itself. Kai regarded our father coolly. He suddenly didn't look anything like a boy. His face was planed by shadows, and his fine hair hung over his eyes. "The government is keeping secrets from you," he said.

"What kind of secrets?" our father asked.

"The kind they don't want you to know."

"Well, then, it's probably better we don't."

Our father's smile was a tight line, but Kai didn't smile at all. "The river is the beginning," he said. "If they can't control it, we can start again."

A new beginning, I thought. Without hunger, thirst, or war. A river could be like a time machine: Step into the same place and it was already changed. But I wondered if there could ever be enough water to start again.

Kai watched me from across the table, his eyes lidded low, pupils barely visible. His skin glowed, and his lips gleamed moistly. When he spoke, his voice was soft and low. "Someday," he said softly to me, "I'll take you there."

CHAPTER 4

After that Will and I became obsessed with Kai's river. But no matter how many times we asked, cajoled, or flattered him, Kai wouldn't say anything else. His father had sworn him to silence, and as much as he wanted to impress us, he feared his father more.

But that didn't stop us from trying.

One morning when Kai met us at the bus stop, Will said, "Kai, let's go to the river today!"

Kai said, "You can't just pick up and walk there."

So we knew it was beyond the boundaries of Arch.

Another day I said, "I wish we could take a boat down that river."

And Kai said, "It's not a river for boating."

So we knew the river would be shallow and fast.

In this way we learned things without Kai even knowing. We learned, for example, that the river traversed the border with the Republic of Minnesota—territory thick with pirates. We learned that men had tried to find the river for years but had given up, because they thought it was a myth. We learned that water from the river began in secret places where no man could reach, in high mountain crags and deep valleys protected by violent winds.

But we could not convince Kai to tell us the location.

A month passed. Our mother got no better. Our father seemed more tired and haggard than before. The days got shorter but no cooler. Merchants draped yellow, gold, and red banners across their windows to remind us of autumn, but they couldn't disguise the monochromatic sameness of the earth and sky. The wind blew harder, and no dry shower could remove the grit permanently embedded beneath our nails and stuck in our skin itself.

Each morning I saw Kai at the bus stop when I went to school, and he was waiting there when Will and I returned. He seemed bored and restless but refused to go to school, because he didn't have to. "They don't teach you anything there," he said. "Nothing worth knowing."

I disagreed. I had learned a lot in school—about butterflies and sand worms; about drainage and absorption; about how water is made of gases that float in the air.

"If you don't go to school, they'll send you straight to the army," I said.

"Will's going to the army," Kai countered.

At least Will's service was only for twelve months. The kids who dropped out of school ended up in the army for years—or worse. Without a job on the outside, or a sponsor, they had nothing to leave for and few reasons for the army to release them.

"Anyway, I have a job. I work for my father," Kai reminded me.

It had been two months since I met him, and I still hadn't seen Kai do any work for his father. But he insisted he was there when his father needed him, and I didn't know enough about the drilling business to recognize if that was just an excuse.

We were walking in the direction of my building, the only ones on the road for miles. In the distance we could see the collapsed facade of a shopping mall: gaping bricks and metal rebar. There weren't enough people to keep buying things, and most businesses had been shuttered or moved back to the central core. Scavengers had picked over the most valuable materials, and the rest of the building was slowly falling into a heap. That was what it looked like all across Arch—and across the entire republic, as far as I could tell. People gathered in close proximity to one another, and anything unprotected was left to criminals and the elements.

Everything fell apart. That was the only constant.

In nine months I would lose my brother to the army. I couldn't bear thinking about what would happen once he left home. He promised he would be fine, but I knew boys left all the time and were scarred forever. If anything happened to Will, I didn't know if I could go on.

And what of Kai?

When I thought of him, I felt a sudden flush creep up my neck. I cast a sidelong glance at him, but he didn't seem to notice. He didn't look anything like the dark and muscular heroes in the romance screens I sometimes read. Besides, I was too young for a boyfriend—that's what my parents had said—even though plenty of girls my age were pairing up. There was one boy last year who had followed me around, but he was creepy and left me alone when Will threatened to beat him up. With Kai, however, I grew more flustered as we walked farther and didn't hear when he asked if he could come over.

"If you'd like," I said after he repeated his question. "My father should be home," I added, in case he got the wrong idea.

We entered the grounds of our complex, passing the empty guard station and the useless and crumbling concrete barriers. Long ago these buildings had been built for retirees who needed security and extra care. But these days few people lived long enough to retire, and there was no money for their care anyway. The guards disappeared first, followed by the upkeep and maintenance. Now we patched our own walls and prayed that the electric wiring would not fail.

Kai climbed the steps ahead of me, his calves outlined against the thin fabric of his trousers. He rang the buzzer, and my father welcomed us. He offered us a snack of crackers and soy cheese, which Kai was happy to accept. We ate in the living room and played board games. The wi-screen glowed softly in the background, playing its constant stream of news, entertainment, and information. We ignored it. It was too early for homework, and I never had much anyway. Will returned, and the three of us swapped stories while Will tried to extract more information about the river.

Soon this became our regular schedule. Our father would leave the door unlocked with a plate of cheese and crackers at the table. Most of the time he would greet us in the kitchen, but sometimes he would let us be. Kai and I grew comfortable with his absence, and I almost forgot the tension of having a boy in my home without a chaperone. At the end of every day, when the black limousine arrived outside our building, Kai seemed reluctant to leave. More than once our father took pity and invited him to dinner. Then we would prolong our game-playing or storytelling until it was finally time for me to do my homework. When Kai was long gone, I'd take a dry shower, set out my clothes for the morning, and read from my mother's collection of *Great Books of the Twentieth Century*: a ten-volume set with torn paper pages, cracked bindings, and scribbled pen markings—the only bound paper volume in our home.

"Poor boy," our father would say.

"He's not poor," said Will.

But we knew what he meant. We just had to look into the bedroom to imagine what it must be like to lose your mother at an early age. Kai feigned indifference, but I understood better than he thought I did. When I tried to get him to talk about his mother, he shrugged and said he really didn't remember her. He wouldn't say much about his father either except that he traveled a lot. Although he was open about his diabetes and showed me the workings of his insulin pencil, he didn't talk much about the disease. He only spoke about the mechanics of treating himself.

Mostly we talked about scavenging, and adventure, and places we wanted to see. Kai mentioned the giant Arctic Ocean—so large it had swallowed Iceland and most of Greenland. I said I'd always wanted to see the Great Dam of China. We played board games, word games, and number games. Kai had a stunning memory and could always recall where a card was hidden or when a piece was last played. He won most of our contests and could even beat Will in Counts, a card game that required a quick hand and an even quicker mind for numbers.

When Kai went home, Will and I stayed up late speculating

about him. Will said Kai feared his father and the burden of keeping the river secret. I said Kai missed his mother and was lost without her. Will teased me and said I was falling for him. I told him I wasn't interested in boys—especially not one whose father wouldn't even let us visit his home. But long after we stopped talking, I would lie in bed thinking about the way Kai's pale hair fell in front of his eyes, and how he bent his head as if he were praying when he listened to me talk.

One weekend morning our father surprised us with three passes to the gaming center. It was a place we begged to go but usually could not afford—ever since we had gone to a party there last year, going back was all we talked about. It was a lukewarm dry Saturday with no rain in sight, but suddenly the day seemed full of promise. Our father explained that he had traded some of Kai's water for the passes, but I noticed no water was missing. We didn't question our good fortune, however; we just took the passes and assured our father we would take Kai along.

In five minutes we were dressed and ready to go—but it took another thirty minutes to reach Kai on the wireless. First we had no signal. Then we had a signal but no response. Finally Kai wi-texted us back, and we made arrangements to meet. We couldn't use our pedicycles, because Kai didn't have one, and the black limousine was with his father—so our father told Will he could take our car. Will jumped at the chance.

Kai was waiting outside his building when we arrived, looking as indifferent as he had the first morning we met. But he grinned broadly when he saw Will driving and actually skipped a step or two on his way to the car. "Cool wheels," he said when he climbed inside, although the old car was anything but, and that made us all laugh. Driving anything was unusual, with gasoline so hard to come by and the electric grid so unreliable. Will sat a little higher in the driver's seat as we headed down the road.

Main Street was rutted and derelict. Most of the old stores had been shuttered or reconstructed to sell the things we still bought: tarps, basins, dried beans, soy bread, and small construction equipment. There were five hardware stores but no drugstore; three gun shops but no bank. The signs of older times could still be seen on the facades of sealed buildings: Gap, Starbucks, Abercrombie & Fitch—merchants that had sold things people didn't necessarily need but always wanted.

The gaming center was in the middle of town next to the water reclamation park. It had been built from the ruins of the old government building that had been bombed when Illinowa declared its independence from the national government in Washington, DC—back when there were fifty states and not six republics. The chief administrator had his office on the top floor, and whatever government existed in Arch conducted its business upstairs.

Will swung the car around the front and parked in the open lot. Our father had given us credit chips, and though Kai certainly didn't need one, he accepted his graciously. We dashed from the car as soon as Will switched it off and entered the center to the hum of the venti-unit and the buzz of generators, consoles, and players.

Although the front of the center was open to the street, the rest of the building was windowless, which reduced the glare on the consoles. In place of windows, the owners had painted murals: lush forests, mist rising from the trees, exotic animals frolicking in the underbrush. The effect was both exhilarating and melancholy, but after a while the feeling wore off, replaced by something like yearning. This made the gamers play harder and longer, seeking the narcotic of the games. It was, of course, the reason the center was decorated this way. Gamers checked in, but they didn't check out until they'd spent their last credit chips.

While the center had its share of children and teens, there were also groups of shakers—men, mostly—who looked as if they had been playing all night. Like many older people, their hands shook from years of thirst. They also had the wild-eyed look of drug addicts, with unkempt hair and clothing they appeared to have slept in. They swiped their game passes in front of the machines like bots, one mechanized sweep after another. Even when they won, their eyes remained glazed and skittery. One victory, another free game, was meaningless. All that mattered was the drug itself. The chief administrator himself was said to be an avid fan and could be found here with his cronies long after dark.

Kai tapped me on the arm. "Shootout," he said.

Will had already run off to play the driving games he liked best. I could see him at the pedals of a race car, both hands working intensely to control the course. He didn't even notice us as we walked past, but I kept him within sight.

Kai was a terrible shot. His skill with numbers was no substitute for sharp eyesight. We played five times in a row, and I beat him every game. Losing, however, did not dim his fun. He screeched and whooped and hollered. As I moved my men to avoid his rockets, he simply sat in the open and took my fire. If he had a strategy, it was to fire furiously and indiscriminately, hoping to overcome with quantity what he could not with quality.

"That was fun!" he said. "Double or nothing." His face was flushed, and he had pushed his hair above his forehead.

"You already owe me more credit chips than you have."

"We'll bet something else."

"Like what?"

"What do you want?"

What did I want? He looked at me expectantly as I tried to sort the confusing puzzle that was my mind. But I couldn't say, so I just said, "Okay, one more game, but then we play something else."

I beat him for the sixth time, and he teased me, calling it beginner's luck. It wasn't luck, I told him, if your aim was true.

We played another game called Geyser where the object was to find water and make it emerge in a powerful jet. The higher it sprayed, the more points you got. I didn't like wasting all that water—even in a game—and I quit after two tries. Kai played three more times by himself, and I wandered through the arcade. There was a YouToo! booth where you could film yourself, add music or mash in other clips, and post videos on the wireless. Two girls performed a clumsy dance routine which they immediately uploaded and viewed on one of the big screens that broadcast a continuous stream of content to anyone with a wireless. Although most homes lacked the technology to broadcast, nearly everyone had a wi-screen for watching and texting. In a matter of minutes, they received ten thousand views and a rating of 1.2 out of 5. Disappointed, the girls insisted on making another video, and I moved on.

A group of boys was crowded behind Will, cheering him on as he set a new high score on Death Racer. Nearby three girls tried to catch the boys' attention. Over by Kai two men in identical blue shirts and black trousers played their own game of Geyser. They had a terrible time figuring out how to play, and their eyes wandered from the screen. It was a waste of credit, I thought; at least they could step aside and let someone else have a turn. But their low scores failed to dim their addiction to losing.

I made my way to Will. He stopped playing to chat with me. This earned me admiring stares from some of the boys and glares from the girls. Will asked if I wanted to race against him, but I knew better than to compete with him at his best event. Instead I suggested he race Kai.

The boys chose their cars. Kai picked a lime-green electric coupe, while Will chose a velvet-blue hydro racer. The cars were steered by two hand paddles; speed was controlled by a foot pedal. Another pedal shifted gears. The course Will selected was an arctic tundra populated by polar bears and baby seals—animals that had once lived where the ground was still frozen. The gun sounded, and Will flew over the landscape, his racer dodging snowdrifts and navigating sub-zero waterways. Kai slipped and skidded on the curvy road, crashing several times into icy mountainsides. Once he went straight through a colony of seals, losing thousands of points for each seal he hit.

But Will and Kai hooted loudly as if they were engaged in a neck-and-neck race instead of a blowout. Their excitement spread to the small crowd of teens who had gathered around them. The girls, who had figured out Will was my brother, wanted to know where we lived and what classes we took. The boys shouted advice to Kai, giving him tips on how to avoid the treacherous roads and packs of bears who tried to ambush him. I couldn't stop smiling. It was more fun than we'd had in a long time. It didn't matter that it was just a game—and not even a very good one. Playing together, being there with Kai and my brother and a group of kids I could imagine were friends, made me forget that our mother lay sick in her bed, dreadfully, inexplicably sick. The narcotic of the game worked its magic, and we were drawn inside.

The cars raced toward the finish line. Over and under, around and through. Will was unbeatable and unstoppable, and I was proud to be his sister.

Then I had an uncomfortable sensation, a prickling at the back of my neck, as if someone were watching me. From the corner of my eye, I saw the two men in the blue shirts staring at us, heads angled low, gazes slanted in our direction. They seemed unnaturally interested, with eyes for no one else in the room.

But when I turned, the men were gone, and I wondered whether I had seen them at all.

CHAPTER 5

The next afternoon Kai wi-texted me to see if I wanted to go scavenging. In the short hills behind his apartment were the remains of an old mill. It had been abandoned in the Great Panic, before we were born. The factory was now a decaying agglomeration of empty buildings, busted silos, and broken-down trucks. Lizards and snakes coiled in the ruins. Our father had warned us never to go there—he claimed there were diseases and dangers— but Kai said it was safe.

It was Sunday, and Will was at water mission class. This summer he would have to spend a month bringing water to less fortunate towns. It didn't matter that we barely had enough water ourselves; the government ordered public service, and there was little choice but to obey. Will said it was just an excuse to get free labor, but even he didn't dare risk defiance. There were "education camps" where they took people who objected and taught them social responsibility. The "lessons" left them damaged and disfigured.

I rode my pedicycle to Kai's complex and locked it outside the front gate. Kai was waiting at the end of the drive. He smiled with one side of his mouth when he saw me and gave a small wave with his hand. Whenever I saw him standing like that, face poised in careful expectation, my heart went out to him. There was something cautious, something held back, in his smile. Drillers trusted no one, and their children learned to be wary and shrewd.

Kai led me through the scraggly cactus-like plants that survived for months without water. He didn't say much, so I kept all the questions to myself. The hills were gradual and gentle, but I soon tired of walking uphill. We stopped for a few minutes, and he gave me a sealed bottle of water that was sweet and still cold. We sat on the side of a concrete barrier overgrown with a grayish lichen that brushed off on our clothes. I drank, and then Kai drank. Our feet kicked up dust.

Before the Great Panic, the mill had produced cornmeal and flour that was shipped across the country. But once the Canadians had dammed the rivers and the lower states began fighting over the trickles that remained, there wasn't enough water for any industry, let alone something as water-intensive as milling. The snow masses and ice packs were gone, victims of warmer temperatures and higher sea levels. The aquifers and surface lakes had dried up or had been polluted. Forests were denuded, wetlands drained. Fresh, drinkable water was in the hands of a very few whose grip grew tighter as the world grew drier.

In truth there hadn't been enough water for years. Our father told us the story they wouldn't tell in school. Rain fell, but it couldn't replenish what was gone. Growing populations made shortages worse. Although the planet was mostly water, less than one-tenth of one percent was drinkable. Riots broke out in the cities. Countries divided into factionalized republics. Wars erupted along their borders. In the aftermath hundreds of millions had died—most from disease and malnutrition. The Great Panic punctuated what men already knew but still somehow refused to accept: the world had run out of water.

"Where do you think the workers went?" I asked. "After the mill shut down?"

Kai shook his head. "There was nowhere to go."

"The planes never bombed it."

"They didn't need to."

He held out his hand to help me up. We continued climbing until we reached the entrance to the old mill. We knew it was the entrance, because part of a broken sign still hung above the ground. Otherwise we would not have recognized it. Wooden and steel beams blocked our passage, and a tangled mass of circuitry dangled from the ceiling like webbing.

Kai said the factory had so much power that the workers never turned off the lights and used the venti-units all night long, even when the buildings were empty. I already knew this from school, but I let Kai lecture me. He said water ran through the pipes that didn't need to be filtered or treated; it could be drunk right out of the tap. This wasn't entirely true. There were giant treatment plants that purified water and added chemicals like chlorine to kill bacteria. I had seen the holos in the archive. Still, things were safer then, and no one got sick just from taking a shower.

Kai held my hand the entire time he talked. Neither of us said anything about it, but I could feel his heart beating in the pulse of his palm. I wondered if this made me his girlfriend. When the girls in school got boyfriends, they usually wore a locket or an old article of the boy's clothing. Maybe, I thought, that's what the water was. I held tight to the empty bottle.

We threaded our way through the beams and wires. At each step Kai cautioned me to avoid a hole, a nail, a plank. Finally we emerged into the center of the factory floor. The old milling machines hunkered like animals, all rusted gears and broken parts. They had run on diesel fuel, which was refined and processed from oil sucked up from deep within the ground. But oil was too precious now to burn in a machine. These days it was rationed and used only to power tanks, jets, and the cars of wealthy men like Kai's father. It was hard to believe oil had ever been so plentiful that people could burn it whenever they chose. But so many of the old ways were wasteful, like letting water spray onto the streets for no other reason than to run around beneath it on a hot day.

I thought about the other costs involved in milling grain. Not only were there oil and electricity for the machines, trucks, venti-units, lights, and refrigerators, but there was all the water to grow the grain in the first place. Millions of hectares of farmland were devoted to corn, soybeans, wheat, and rye. The government built thousands of kilometers of aqueducts that took water from rivers halfway across the country and brought it to the farms. There were places in the desert that suddenly bloomed with vineyards and orange groves. Towns without water were transformed into green paradises where people played games on tracts of perfect grass. Entire cities sprang from dust and clay, their spires reaching into the sky and their roots deep into the earth. They sucked up water as if it were their birthright and spat out sewage back onto the land. There was no limit to Earth's resources—until there wasn't anything left anymore.

We hiked over and around machines as big as trucks. In every building the windows were shattered, and the walls were scoured of anything valuable. Floors and ceilings had collapsed, and splintered trusses lay everywhere. Some of the interior offices were intact, but they were completely empty of furniture, paneling, and anything else that would burn. The copper wiring had been stripped away, and the machines had ben robbed clean of fuel for use during the cold winters that followed.

The rear of the factory was open to the hills behind it. It was here that the trucks stopped to fill up with their loads of milled grain. There was a road that looped around the buildings, then made its way beneath a stack of elevators. The road was badly eroded—more sand and rock than concrete—but it was flat and clear of debris. We walked through the factory and out onto the road, then followed it until we came to a gully that cut the road in two. A short steel bridge had provided passage across, but it lay collapsed in the ditch, the victim of too many crossings and too much time.

"This way," said Kai, stepping down into the ditch. He did not turn around and walked as if he knew where he was leading. It occurred to me then that this trip to explore the mill was not what it appeared: not a random wandering among the ruins, but a planned tour with a knowledgeable guide. Kai walked with purpose, navigating the rutted path like someone who had trudged there before. He released my hand and expected me to follow.

"Where are we going?"

"I want to show you a secret."

We walked about five hundred meters down the gully, and then Kai climbed up the steep side away from the mill. There was no sound except our footsteps. No wind. No shade. Not a cloud in the sky. Everything was brown, burned, dried, or cracked.

"There," he said. He was pointing to a nondescript patch of ground on which there was nothing but some gravel and broken glass.

"There, where?"

"Dig there," he instructed.

I bent down and scratched at the dirt, which came away surprisingly easily in my fingers. It felt soft and slightly wet, as if it had just rained, which was impossible. I dug a little more quickly, and the dirt got wetter, which was definitely impossible.

"Kai?" I looked up at him. For the first time I felt something like fear. We were nearly a kilometer away from the nearest building, and twice that far from any living being. I realized there were so many things I didn't know about this boy. How come we had never seen his father? How did his mother die? Why didn't he go to school? All of his explanations suddenly seemed unbelievable. A boy didn't just stop going to school with his father's blessing or wander abandoned grounds as if he owned them. Eventually the government came to get him, or he went away. But Kai was still here, pointing at the earth.

"It's okay," he said. "Dig."

I scooped deeper into the dirt, which began to come away in soggy lumps. "What is it?" I asked, although I already knew.

"Water," he said.

"How did it get here?"

"There's a spring underground. A small one. It runs right under the mill."

I shook my head. I couldn't believe there was fresh water so close to our home. Yet there it was, trickling through the sand in my fingers. As mysterious as Kai himself.

"Does anyone know?"

Kai shook his head slowly.

"Where...how did you find it?"

He shrugged. "I knew it was there."

Kai's face shone, and the gold in his hair refracted the sunlight. Finding a source of free water was like finding oil—better, even. It could make a person wealthy beyond imagination. But Kai didn't seem to care. He regarded me with drowsy eyes below his bangs.

"You could be rich," I said.

"There's not even enough water to fill a cistern."

"There might be."

"There isn't."

I placed my fingers to my lips and tasted the water that came from the ground. It was sandy and gritty, but there was no chemical aftertaste and no brackish residue. I wasn't worried about poisons or toxins, because I could tell it was real water, filtered deep in the earth. I scooped up another handful and let it wash over my face, closing my eyes as the drops cut cool rivulets down my cheeks.

At first I thought I was dreaming. And then I realized the lips on my own were Kai's. He pressed against me, his warm breath washing my face like night. The air chopped and eddied, and I felt like I was falling into something deep and bottomless from which there could be no rescue. When I opened my eyes, his eyes were bright and large before me. "You shouldn't," I said.

"Sorry," he said.

"Stop, I mean."

I leaned back into him, and we kissed again. My lungs inhaled him, and his breath was my breath. We kissed until I was dizzy from it, and swirls of color patterned beneath my eyelids. When we stopped, the softness of his mouth lingered like buzzing. I touched my lips, and they felt warm and liquid—not at all like the dry chapped feeling of wind and sun. Kai's gaze mirrored mine, and I looked back into his eyes as if I could see my own emotions reflected in them. They were a clear limpid blue, without a hint of gray.

We stood that way for a moment, eyes locked, hands clasped, and then he moved toward me. This time I stepped back, and his lips brushed my cheek.

"I'm sorry. I'm all confused," I said. "I mean, it's not like I don't want to keep on, but I don't—I don't know what it means."

Kai nodded as if he understood. Another boy might have pushed himself on me or tried to change my mind. Kai simply covered the small hole I had dug, patting the sand back into place. "Want to see the rest of the site?" he asked.

He took my hand, and we continued our tour of the dry hills and dusty grounds. He showed me the tiny lizards that lived deep in the sand and were able to withstand the winter. He pushed aside broken pilings and showed me colonies of ants that feasted off water in the decayed wood. But nothing else made any impression on me during the rest of our afternoon together at the old mill. Later I would regret not asking him more. Part of me wished we could go back to the moment before the kiss. He had become my closest friend—my only real friend besides Will, if I was honest—and I worried what would happen to that friendship if we kept on. But the other part of me felt old enough to continue. He was the first boy for whom I'd felt anything but curiosity, and I didn't know then how to speak my mind about the things I wanted.

It was getting dark by the time we made our way to Kai's building, and I knew my father would not want me cycling home. I called him from the lobby to pick me up. Kai apologized for not inviting me inside, but I understood. Germs spread more easily indoors, and it wasn't worth alarming his neighbors.

We waited together downstairs. Kai's father remained upstairs. The security guards kept their distance. There was a single hard-backed chair, and Kai offered it to me, but I was content to keep standing. An old digital clock on the wall kept time. Minutes blinked slowly past. The intimacy we had shared in the abandoned ruins felt as far away as the buildings themselves. It was as if Kai weren't there, even though he was standing right next to me. I listened intently and could just hear him breathing. I wondered whether he was embarrassed that he had kissed me and wished he hadn't. Then I wondered if the kiss had been any good and if he had kissed many other girls. But he was staring off into the distance, and all I could see in front of him were the walls of the building and a bank of security lights. The lights blinked and flickered, sending their coded messages into the night.

"Kai," I finally said.

"Yes?"

We heard a car honk outside.

"It's my father," I told him.

"Will I see you tomorrow?"

"Sure."

"Tomorrow, then."

My concerns were silly, I told myself as I ran out the door. Kai wasn't upset or disappointed. He was just naturally distracted, like a boy who listened to a different voice. And I knew he trusted me; he had shown me the underground spring. Maybe I wasn't ready to be his girlfriend, but that didn't mean I had to stop seeing him. It didn't mean either that we knew what the weeks or months ahead would bring. I wouldn't be fifteen forever.

That night I told Will nearly everything—except the part about the kiss. I was certain Kai didn't want me to keep a secret from Will. He was my brother, after all. But Will didn't believe me. Everyone knew there was no water for miles, he insisted. We must have come upon a leaking cistern or a buried tank. Will raised his voice, and I raised mine back, and the fight ended with our father coming upstairs to separate us. I decided Will wasn't worth telling anyway. I didn't care about his opinion. It was just as well he didn't believe me.

But the next morning, Will asked about the spring again. I repeated what I had told him, and this time he seemed interested.

"Let's go see it," he said.

"We've got school."

"After school."

"It's behind the old mill."

"We don't have to say where we're going."

I nodded. Of course I wouldn't say anything to our father. Will knew that. He pursed his lips and solemnly shook my hand. I understood then—he was jealous that Kai had shown me the spring. But if he suspected anything else, he didn't let on.

The school day seemed to take forever. Every word the teachers said hung in the air as if coated with thick paste. I tried to get my mind around the words, but they landed back on my desk with a splat. They were unrecognizable, and my brain was dulled with the effort of trying to discern their meaning. I forced myself to sit upright, but all I could think about was showing Will that patch of wet earth.

Finally the bell rang, and with a whoop, the kids raced down the hallway. Normally I took my time gathering my belongings, but today I joined the others in the mad dash for the buses.

Will was waiting for me. We boarded the bus and sat next to each other without speaking. Other kids jostled for Will's attention, but he ignored them. He gripped the seat in front of him and stared straight ahead. I knew what he was thinking. It was the same thing I had thought when I first saw the spring. A free-flowing source of water could mean more water nearby. More water could mean the aquifers were replenished. Replenished aquifers meant clean water—water that wouldn't have to be purified, treated with harmful chemicals, poisoned. It was water our mother could drink.

Maybe Kai was wrong about there being very little water. He couldn't know for certain. Geologists would have to drill and test. Sometimes the water could be a kilometer or more below the surface. A trickle could mean huge reservoirs underneath. These were complicated matters to be divined by scientists and hydrologists.

But when we got off the bus, Kai wasn't there. At first I assumed he was just late. I realized how much I had counted on him being there every day; not seeing him was jarring, like walking past the same building and suddenly noticing it was gone and there was a huge hole where it once stood. In the last two months, I had almost forgotten the time before he existed, and now his absence felt like a sharp ache. The longer we waited, however, the more we realized Kai wasn't coming. I wasn't worried; not yet.

"We could go without him," I suggested.

"What's the fun in that?"

"He would be upset," I agreed.

"Let's go find him."

It wasn't far to the Wellington Pavilion. We got our pedicyles from the locked storage room and cycled down the familiar road. Several cars passed, the drivers steering wide to avoid us. The sun hung low in the sky, a dull orange-brown ball filtered through haze and dust. Finally we saw the triple spires of the Wellington Pavilion over the next hill and picked up our pace. Will raced me to the driveway, then let me win.

The guards stopped us at the gate.

"We're going to see Kai," said Will.

"Kai?" asked one of the guards.

"Tall, about my height," said Will. "Blond. Hangs around outside all day."

"You know me," I said to the guard. "I've been here before."

The guard shook his head. "You got a certification?"

Of course we didn't have our certificates with us. I looked at Will to see what he would do next. I was certain he would find a way to talk himself inside. Instead he shrugged and said, "Oh, well, I guess we'll see him back at school." He walked off, pushing his cycle, and I followed.

"Will!" I hissed. "Why didn't you say something?"

"Can't talk sense to a guard," said Will. "Follow me."

Although the Wellington Pavilion was one of the fanciest housing complexes, it too suffered from a lack of regular maintenance. Without water it was difficult to fix nearly anything. Road crews used dry-crete, a waterless cement, but it crumbled easily in the heat. Asphalt was practically nonexistent, because even petroleum substitutes were impossible to find. As I followed my brother, circling the compound, we soon came to a part of the fence that had rusted out, and the concrete had disintegrated below. We leaned our cycles against a pole, and Will pushed at the fence. It quickly broke away in his hands. "In here," he said.

The space was just big enough to slip through. Will went first, and I followed. So much for security.

"Three-B," I said, remembering Kai's apartment number.

We snuck across the sandy lot, colored green to resemble grass, although it didn't look anything like it. We didn't see a soul. This was what it was like to be rich: You didn't have to leave your apartment, risking the outside air and the lack of water. You lived in a secure compound with guards who stopped visitors at the gate. When people came to visit, they had to be certified and cleared, or else they snuck in beneath the torn and tangled barbed wire.

At the stairwell Will pulled at the door, and it opened easily—either the lock had been removed or it was broken. We climbed three flights, our footsteps echoing eerily in the dim passage. A thin coat of sand made the banister gritty, and several times I had to wipe my hands on my trousers to clean them.

Something was wrong. We could tell as soon as we reached the third floor. A breeze blew down the hallway—not the familiar and comforting air of a venti-unit, but the hot, dry breath from outside. Sure enough, when we reached the end of the hallway, we could see an apartment door swinging open on a single hinge. Will slowed and signaled for quiet, although I wouldn't have made a sound even if I could. We tiptoed the last several feet to the apartment door, and then Will peered around inside.

The intake of his breath was like a sharp cry.

I eased behind him and looked over his shoulder. The apartment appeared trashed, as if someone had set about to wreck it. Broken lamps on the floor. Shattered windows. An overturned table in the kitchen. Dishes scattered beside it. A rank odor, like spoiled food, filled the air. It was too much to take in at once, and for several seconds I didn't see what had made Will cry out.

A bloodied body lay face down near the doorway to the bedrooms. I recognized him instantly, and my stomach turned: Martin the bodyguard, the machine pistol still in his hand, his broken sunglasses lying about two meters away. I noticed bullet holes in the walls now, and empty shell casings on the floor.

"Kai?" I called. "Kai?"

But my voice echoed hollowly in the empty apartment. Kai was gone.

CHAPTER 6

The laser torches lit the hallway in streaks of purple and red. Will saw them first while I rummaged through a stack of paper and notebooks on a desk made of real wood.

"RGs," he hissed.

RGs were members of the Republic Guard who were armed with high-tech gear. Feared and loathed in equal measure, they protected the republic's border and what was left of its infrastructure. But there wasn't enough time to wonder why the RGs were here. Their arrival was never a good thing. There was a dead body and spent ammunition and two kids old enough to be saboteurs. We had to flee before we were trapped.

The lights danced across the open doorway. Will and I huddled in the back of the small room that served as Kai's father's office. There was a second door that led into a bath, and from there into Kai's bedroom. We tiptoed to the bathroom. Outside we could hear the guards' electronic communications. They spoke in clipped military language, most of which I couldn't understand, but I clearly heard them say we were cornered in the building.

The only thing that saved us was Kai's medicine kit on the side of the sink. As I stopped to examine it, the RGs entered the bedroom.

They would surely have seen us if we had continued into the room. Instead Will bumped into me and we both froze behind the door. Then we quickly retraced our steps to the office, back through the living room to the front hallway—and out the open door.

Two men stood just inside the perimeter of the fence by the front gate. They were dressed in the same blue shirts as the men I had seen at the gaming center, and each carried an automatic weapon.

Will raised a finger to his lips. He signaled toward the hole in the fence. We scurried quickly in the twilight and slipped through the opening before anyone noticed. Then we leapt on our pedicycles and rode silently like madmen until we were within sight of our building.

"We can't stay here," gasped Will as we stopped to catch our breath about fifty meters from our front door.

"What do you mean? Where else can we go?"

He nodded at the security cameras mounted on nearly every building corner. Of course: the cameras at the Wellington Pavilion had filmed our arrival. It wouldn't take long for the RGs to review the logs and identify us in the database.

"But we didn't do anything!" I protested.

"It won't look that way."

I was still gripping Kai's medicine kit. Now I looked inside. Four neat, contoured insulin reservoirs were secured in an insulated pouch next to two boxes of blood-testing strips and a spare adapter for the injector pencil.

"He left without his insulin," I said.

"Why would he do that?"

"He didn't do it," I said. "They took him."

"We don't know that. He could have been running."

"You saw the bodyguard! Do you think he shot himself?"

"Maybe he got shot protecting Kai and his father, and they got away."

"Then where's the blood and the other bodies?"

"Could be no one else was wounded."

But Will knew I was right. No matter how desperate Kai's situation, he wouldn't leave voluntarily without his insulin. It was a death sentence.

"We have to help him, Will."

"We can't go to the Guard, or the army. They'll be looking for us."

"Then we have to go ourselves."

"Don't be crazy. They'll have guns, and we don't even know who *they* are."

"If we stay here, the Guard will arrest us. You said so yourself." My voice cracked; my throat was bone dry.

"And what do we do if we find him? Shoot our way inside?"

"If we have proof, the Guard will come. Especially if there's money in it."

Will frowned. But he knew the Republic Guard would help a wealthy driller if we had a holo or even an audiogram—anything they could link to bank records.

"We should tell Dad," said Will. "Just in case."

I couldn't believe Will was suggesting this. Our father would never let us leave. I told Will he was scared and making excuses. He said he was being rational and weighing the risks. The more we argued, the more forceful I became. For once I was the leader and Will the reluctant follower. He may have had logic, but I had passion and desire.

"If we lose Kai, we lose the river," I said. "We lose everything."

The lights had come on outside our building, and soon the grid would shut down. Will's face was smeared with dust and grime from the ride, and I assumed I looked the same. My lips stung, and my hair felt matted with sweat and sand. But I felt exhilarated and prepared for anything. Will's uneven grin told me he felt the same way.

"We don't know where to start," he said.

"Yes, we do."

I retrieved Kai's father's notebooks from my side basket. In them he had detailed the site of an old well that was about forty kilometers from Arch. I couldn't understand all his notations, but it looked like he had found water there. If so, there were plenty of suspects who would kidnap him for the information.

We cleaned up as best we could outside. Luckily our father was making dinner for our mother. He didn't notice as we tiptoed past him to the bath. By the time he returned from the bedroom, I had set the table, and we were sitting in front of our plates looking as innocent as we could. I have no idea what we talked about. Every bump and sound made me jerk with worry that the RGs had arrived. We could only pray that it would take them some time to review the tapes and run a data scan, because it was too dark now to cycle on the roads. I don't think I slept a wink, and I know Will didn't, because I could hear him thrashing and pacing in his room.

We left before dawn. We wrote a note explaining that we had

gone to school early with a friend's parent for water team. It was something our father could have checked, but he had plenty of other things to worry about. It was not the first time we had gone to school early, nor the first time someone had given us a ride.

Our plan was to return before dark. We had goggles, masks, and sunshields. The wind could be fierce on the open road, and the shields would also protect against flying sand. Will brought some food, two liters of water in a saddlebag, and his old instant holo-camera. I brought my credit chip. I had saved my weekly allowance for most of the year, and although it was only fifty credits, that was enough to buy four meals and another liter of water and still leave something for an emergency. I also had Kai's medicine kit with his insulin and injector.

As Will calculated it, we could ride north on our pedicycles at about fifteen kilometers an hour. It should be no more than three hours to reach the well. If we were wrong, and Kai wasn't there, we could return before our father knew we had gone. If there was any trouble, we had the camera and could send the holos by wireless. The RGs could come within an hour. At least that was the plan.

But we made two mistakes. The first was that we assumed our pedicycles could withstand the grueling ride over forty-two kilometers of broken road. The cycles were meant for short trips—the market, school, a friend's apartment complex. They were not meant for dirt and gravel roads that had not been repaired in years and were littered with old car parts, scrap metal, rubber, and glass. We made it about fourteen kilometers before I got my first flat. Will fixed the tire with the repair kit and some compressed air, but the second flat could not be repaired. The metal rim had separated from the tire, and no amount of pounding and banging would straighten it out. We had to abandon the cycle on the side of the road, and I climbed behind Will on his cycle.

The extra weight, however, soon exhausted Will. He couldn't pedal for both of us, and we stopped frequently so he could catch his breath. Then he got a flat too and ran out of compressed air while fixing it. Now his front tire was half-inflated, and that made pedaling even more difficult. I offered to trade places, but I didn't have the strength to cycle more than a kilometer. It took us six hours instead of three to reach the site of the old well. Neither of us said anything about how long it would take to get back.

Our second mistake was to think that there might be water at a place so desiccated and lost. The well had been drained years ago, and the coating of dust everywhere quickly told us there had been few visitors. Cracked and parched earth was all that remained where there had once been soft loamy soil. No water had flowed since at least the Great Panic, if not before.

Kai was not here and probably never had been. Whatever the notations meant in his father's notebook, the well wasn't related to the kidnapping. Our lengthy trip had been foolish—and needlessly risky. As it was, darkness was coming, and we had no way to reach our father without a wireless signal. It was all my fault for suggesting we come here in the first place.

"They must have taken him farther north," said Will. His voice was barely a whisper.

"Maybe. Wherever they went, they've got a twenty-hour head start."

"Don't even think about it. We'll never catch them. Not with the pedicycle."

"But Will!"

He shook his head. "The only way to help them is to turn ourselves in to the Guard."

"They'll lock us up."

"It's our only chance."

Then my eye caught it: the faintest glimmer, a slight twinkle in the sun that I might not have seen if the light hadn't caught it in just the right way.

I picked up the syringe and showed it to Will.

"He was here," I said.

"It's just an old needle."

"No. It's a backup for his injector. He told me. If his pencil runs out, he can always use a syringe and a bottle. He was here."

Will rolled the needle between thumb and forefinger like a valuable piece of silver. "There must be tracks," he said.

"Yes," I said, encouraging him.

"But which way?"

He walked backward slowly, his eyes fixed on the ground, scanning every inch of surface. I followed, trying to force my vision to see through the sand and dirt. If someone had been here, the wind would have covered the tracks quickly. And although the well looked untouched, half a day's sandstorm would make anything look ancient.

At first the growl in the distance sounded like a storm. It came with very little warning. But as it got closer, the growl grew deeper, like a wild animal. Will straightened and tensed beside me.

"What is it?" I asked.

"Trucks," he said. "Lots of them."

"Could it be Kai?"

Our view of the horizon was restricted, because the ground sloped away from where we stood. Several low-slung buildings also blocked our sight line. We could hear the trucks roaring, but we were otherwise blind. The sound morphed into different pitches—some high and whining, others low and rumbling: A convoy of vehicles heading for the front lines, or escaping with kidnap victims? Or maybe both…?

Then the roar ceased. This was unusual, because the vehicles in a convoy would never shut off their engines—even *I* knew that. In an ambush they would not be able to flee immediately. This was someone who was not afraid of an ambush, for whom fuel mattered more than fleeing. Neither the army nor the Guard would ever take such a risk. Then Will spotted them.

"Run! Vera, run!"

A dozen or so men dressed in tattered black clothing, bearded and large, appeared over the horizon. They walked with guns extended, poised, and ready to shoot. If these were the men who had kidnapped Kai, we didn't stand a chance.

My legs felt bolted to the earth. I couldn't move. Will grabbed my hand and pulled me away from the road. Behind us I could hear the men yelling and the machines restarting their engines.

"Who are they?" I shouted as I stumbled to keep up with Will.

"Water pirates!" His voice quavered.

I nearly fell down. Water pirates were the worst kind of vigilantes.

They traveled like nomads, stealing water wherever they could find it and selling it to the highest bidder. They owed allegiance to no government and killed all who crossed them.

Will veered off the flattened sands onto rocky terrain, and I followed as fast as I could. We could hear the trucks roaring down upon us and something else in the sky. I looked up and saw a sight I'd seen only once before in my life: a helicopter. Two men with guns squatted in the open hatchway.

"*Stop running!*" an amplified voice commanded.

Will zigzagged, trying to scamper by the biggest rocks to slow the trucks. He kept one arm out for me, and I grabbed it, feeling the muscle in his forearm throbbing with the effort of the chase. We ran clumsily. I feared each step would be my last. I waited for the bullets to rip the air and wondered what it would feel like to be shot. Painful, like a vaccination, or quick and peaceful? Dust and dirt filled my vision, and it was hard to breathe. My lungs burned, and my feet ached from the rocks. But soon the road was a good half-kilometer behind us, and the sound of the trucks had faded. The helicopter, however, kept pace overhead.

"Why are they chasing us?"

"They don't want anyone to know they were here," said Will.

Stealing water was a crime punishable by death. Even wildcatters, like Kai's father, did their drilling with government licenses. Although the army rarely caught them, pirates were executed or sent to camps from which they never returned. Like other "undesirables," they threatened the stability of a fragile republic. But this only made pirates more ruthless and determined never to be captured. They trusted no one and killed those who betrayed them. I ran harder.

Then we heard the dogs.

It was a sound I knew only from the wireless. Dogs were too expensive for most people to own. Unlike cats they drank plenty of water and could not hunt their own food. Left alone they were quickly killed by coyotes, one of the few other animals that survived in the wild. But they were still bred for certain purposes— including hunting runaways.

"Will!"

"I know! I heard them!" he said. "Hurry!"

But the two of us were no match for men with dogs, to say nothing of a helicopter that kept a close watch from the sky. The barking got louder, and the blades of the copter beat the air around us. We ran, but the pirates ran faster. I stumbled, and an arm reached out to grab me. But it wasn't Will's arm. It was tattooed and covered with scars, twisted and gnarled—a pirate's arm.

CHAPTER 7

They cuffed us, then threw us in the back of a truck. Will tried to protest, but one of the men raised a revolver and silenced him. We headed north.

Through the·slats in the side of the truck, I could see orange and violet bands of light as the sun crossed the afternoon sky. The truck banged roughly along the road, and the bands kept shifting and blinding me. I nudged Will, but he ignored me. He had been silent since the pirates forced us into the truck, and my efforts to get him to talk failed. He had a bruise on one arm where a pirate had grabbed him roughly, and every now and then, his hand went to the bruise, stroking it like a painful memory.

Two men sat with us, their guns held tightly across their laps as if they thought one of us might make a run for it. But even if there were somewhere to run, leaping from the back of a speeding truck wasn't the first thing on my mind. The guns were big, the men were even bigger, and the helicopter was still overhead. I could tell Will was thinking about running. I wanted to tell him we were approaching the northern boundary and the Republic of Minnesota.

Minnesota had once been loosely bound to the lower republics, but it declared its secession after the Great Panic, and the army made no effort to stop it. Since then, it sold water to the other republics, but it stuck by its declaration and even sent troops to the border to prevent immigrants without proper documentation from sneaking through.

I knew we were getting close because the truck slowed and the road got rougher. From the angle of the sun, I knew the direction we were going and how long we had been driving. It all added up to a border crossing into the powerful republic. There was no way a convoy of pirates could get across the border, however, and I wondered what the men had planned. Will sensed it too because after hours of silence, he sat up straight and cocked his head as if he were listening intently.

"*Minnesota*," I whispered to him.

He nodded and turned to the pirates, speaking for the first time. "You'll never get across."

The pirates seemed surprised to discover a real live boy in the back of the truck with them. One of them asked Will to repeat what he had said.

"They'll stop you at the border. You don't have papers."

"Don't you worry about the border," said the pirate. "We'll get through just fine."

"I don't see how."

"It's not for you to be worrying."

"If they shoot us all, I'll be worried."

I couldn't believe Will was talking this way to a pirate. The pirate couldn't either. "For a boy who's a prisoner of pirates," he said, "you're pretty cheeky."

Will shrugged. "I'm just saying if we all get killed, what good is kidnapping us?"

"If we're all killed, what good is worrying about it?" The pirate snickered and slapped his companion on the back, and Will was quiet for a while.

The truck continued to slow, and the men grew more alert. I couldn't hear the helicopter anymore, and I guessed it had flown away so as not to get close to the border and risk being shot down. I didn't think Minnesota had an air force, but it definitely had air defenses, and it wouldn't let an unknown copter cross its skies. I heard the radio crackle in the front seat and some voices blurt forth in a different language. The driver responded, and there was some more crackling. The truck bumped loudly over a couple of barriers, and each time, we landed hard on our rumps. Finally it slowed and then came to a complete stop. All was silent.

The radio burst forth again in that strange language. The driver answered, and another voice joined in as well. Then more silence.

I strained to hear something, and I could just make out boots crunching against gravel outside. I pressed my face to the truck's side, and I could hear the engine ticking as it cooled. More boots crunched, and a new voice called out. There was some muffled talking, and some more boots joined in. Then a hand grabbed me by the scruff of the neck and pulled me away from the side.

"What's so interesting?" asked the pirate who had spoken to Will. He was large, bearded, and bald, and his arms were covered with tattoos.

I shrugged. My ears burned.

"You're wasting your time snooping," said the pirate.

"You're going to buy your way across." The idea came to me in a flash.

"You're a smart missy."

How else did pirates move about so freely? They couldn't fight their way across, because they were outnumbered. Plus all those boots outside meant people talking about something important: money, water, or both.

"But how do you know they won't shoot you once you're across?" I asked. "No, that would be stupid," I said, answering my own question.

The pirate nodded. "We wash their hands, and they wash ours."

"Is it illegal to steal water if they don't arrest you?" I asked.

"Not if you pay them enough." The pirate smiled widely, big gaps where his teeth should be.

Perhaps this was the way things worked in the shaker world. The rules only applied to people who couldn't afford different rules. If you had money, you had choices—like pirates crossing the border freely, or Kai not attending school, or the WABs drinking clean water. If you didn't, you had only chances.

The talking stopped, and then the truck's engine growled to life. The other vehicles joined in, and soon we were moving. I could hear the helicopter overhead again.

"Where are you taking us?"

"Only he knows for sure," the pirate said.

"He? Who?"

But the pirate was silent, and from the glare Will gave me, I knew it was best not to keep asking questions.

We drove for another hour until the sun had completely set. My bottom ached, and my neck was stiff and sore. Will had fallen asleep against my thigh. He awoke with a start when the truck honked loudly three times, followed by two short taps. After a moment an air horn responded with the same sequence. The truck lurched forward, and the sound against the tires was smoother and quieter. After a few minutes, the truck slowed, then stopped again.

"Where are we?"

"Sanctuary," said the pirate.

The men hopped out of the back of the truck and left us inside. I could hear motors shutting down all around and men greeting each other loudly. I tried to stand, but the plastene cuffs the pirates had placed around my ankles made it impossible. I fell and started to cry.

Will put one arm around me. "Shh," he murmured. "It's all right."

"They're going to kill us," I choked out.

"If they were going to kill us, they would have done it already. They could have left us by the side of the road instead of bringing us all the way up here."

I had to admit it would have been easy enough to shoot us and leave us in the road. Pirates did it all the time. "Then why are we here?" I asked.

"I don't know. Let's wait and see. We must have something they want."

I tried to imagine what the pirates might want, but I couldn't. We weren't rich, and we had no water. If the pirates hoped for a ransom, our father barely had enough money for our mother's medicine. He would give them everything, but it wouldn't be enough. Thinking about it only made me cry harder.

"Don't cry, Vera," said Will. He smoothed my hair against the side of my face, outlining a brown parenthesis against my cheek.

"I wish we were home."

"We will go home. I promise."

"I wish we had told the Guard. I'd rather be in jail than here."

Will took a deep breath. "We're hundreds of kilometers from Illinowa. We have to see what the pirates have planned. We need to stay calm, watch, and wait. We'll have our chance."

Of course Will was right again. But I realized clearly for the first time how desperate our plight was. It had been foolish to think we could rescue Kai. Now, wherever he was, it couldn't be worse than being held captive by pirates. Even cannibals were more trustworthy.

Before I could let my fears completely overwhelm me, the doors on the back of the truck burst open, and two new pirates came inside.

"You two," said one of the men, as if there might be two other children in the back of the truck. "Come with me."

Will lifted a leg to show him it was cuffed. The pirate growled, then stomped out. In a moment he returned with wire cutters. "Worthless," he said. Then he snipped clean through our restraints.

We stumbled out of the back of the truck and into a night lit by torches and halo-lights. I blinked and nearly keeled over, but Will caught me. The pirate took me by the other arm, and he marched us across a dirt lot toward a cinder-block building. There were about a half-dozen trucks parked in a circle alongside some heavy machinery. The helicopter had landed nearby. Smoke still trailed from its exhaust, and its blades spun lazily. Men watched as we crossed the lot—dark men, disheveled and dirty. A dog barked, and I instinctively gripped the pirate's hand, then let go. Although I was trembling inside, I made up my mind to refuse to let the pirate know. I held up my head and strode purposefully forward.

The man rapped once on a steel door at the front of the cinder-block building. In a moment the door opened, and he pushed us inside. The dimly lit room was darker than the night, and my eyes were momentarily blind. I could make out a few candles and then soft fabrics hanging from the walls. Music played quietly—acoustic instruments from an earlier era. Even as my eyes adjusted, however, my brain could not. Curtains, candles, and music were the last things I expected from pirates, and they were a stark contrast from the concrete exterior.

"What kind of children walk the open road?" asked a deep voice from the shadows.

"We weren't walking," said Will. "We had our pedicycles."

"Didn't get you very far, did they?"

The voice belonged to a man about our father's age and height. He wore black boots, a gray sweatshirt, and black canvas pants that fit tightly at his waist. He had longish hair, a thick beard, and a tattoo of a small bird on the side of his neck. His nails were clean, and he wore a single yellow band on his left ring finger. His hands were stroking the fur on the heads of two golden-brown dogs.

I stepped back instinctively, but the dogs remained still. "Are you going to kill us?" I asked.

"Kill you? Why would I kill you?"

"You've kidnapped us."

"I haven't kidnapped you. We found you on the road. You would've starved to death if we hadn't picked you up."

"Is that why your men chased us and hunted us down?"

The pirate frowned and stopped petting the dogs. "You ran from them."

"Because they were pirates."

"What do you know about pirates?"

I considered his question. Everything I knew about pirates, I had learned in school. They were dangerous, lawless men, who would do anything to steal water, including killing and maiming. But it was true that I had never met a real pirate, and didn't know anyone who had.

"Pirates steal water," said Will, "water that's meant for other people."

The pirate laughed, deep and rich. His hair bounced on his shoulders like something alive. "Governments steal water," he said, "water that doesn't belong to them."

Will stared at the pirate but didn't say anything else. Water belonged to whoever drilled or refined it, and pirates certainly did neither. They took the water collected through the hard work of others.

"So now what are you going to do with us?" I asked.

"What should I do?" asked the pirate.

"Let us go."

"Can't do that, little sister. How will you get home? It's dangerous out there for children."

Of course the pirate was right. There was nothing but rocks and sand between here and home. Even if we could get back across the border now, we could never walk hundreds of kilometers without water. And even if we could, bandits or coyotes would surely get to us. We were trapped with bad men in a foreign republic. I bit my lip to stop myself from crying again.

"We're not children," said Will, annoyed.

I expected the pirate to laugh, as shakers usually did when kids insisted they were grown up. But instead he did something strange. He raised his head and looked off into the distance as if he could see something there. "No," he said. "Of course not."

"Will you let us go, then?"

The pirate returned his gaze to Will, and then he did laugh. "Do I look like a fool? Let you run straight to the army?"

"We won't. We promise!" said Will.

"A boy's promise. That's pretty."

"It's worth more than a pirate's."

"You have a lot to learn about pirates."

I knew what Will was thinking: The farther we went, the harder it would be to get home. The harder it was to get home, the less likely we were to ever see our parents again—traveling with pirates, no less, who knew where or how far? Twenty-four hours ago we had a plan to rescue Kai. Now *we* needed rescuing.

"We're looking for a boy," said the pirate. "About your age."

"A boy?" repeated Will.

"A boy and his father—a driller."

I opened my mouth, but quickly shut it.

Kai, I thought. *They're looking for Kai.*

CHAPTER 8

The pirate was called Ulysses. He said he was named after an ancient warrior, but I had never heard that tale. I thought of him instead as the king of the pirates. Like a king he rode tall and proud at the wheel in the first truck. He insisted the pirates had no king; they didn't even have a leader. They were wanderers who went wherever the winds and water took them.

"Why do they follow you, then?" I asked.

"They're free not to. They follow me because they want to."

"That still makes you the leader."

"Are we free not to follow you?" asked Will. He sat pressed up against the door. Ulysses was driving, and I was in the middle. The two dogs—Cheetah and Pooch—sat in a small compartment behind us. Cheetah (or maybe it was Pooch) kept poking her head over the divider and sniffing my face. Although the dogs had frightened me when they first tracked us, up close they seemed like large furry dolls that would rather sleep, lick, and sniff than bite. In fact, I knew, dogs had been pets until feeding them made their masters hungry.

"You're children. Children don't have choices."

"That's just what shakers always say."

"They say it because it's true."

I had no idea where we were, except I knew we were traveling north again. The pirates seemed to know what they were doing, because their caravan moved fast—as fast as the broken roads allowed. I counted ten vehicles: three pickups, two jeeps, four tanker cars, and a converted fire truck the pirates used for pumping water. Somewhere overhead, the helicopter followed.

"Do you have children?" I asked.

The pirate was silent for a moment. "No," he said finally.

"Are you married?" asked Will.

"Yes," said Ulysses.

"Where's your wife, then?" I asked.

"You ask a lot of questions," said Ulysses.

I waited for him to say something else, but he did not, so I decided to stay silent as well. I peered out the window over Will's shoulder. Minnesota did not look any different than home. The landscape was brown and dry, and there were broken buildings and cracked roads everywhere. No people; no signs of life. If there was more water here, you certainly couldn't see it from the ground. Minnesota kept its riches well-hidden.

The trucks rumbled northward. I nudged Will, but he ignored me. I occupied myself instead by scanning the horizon for clouds. The sky, however, was perfectly blue, and every time I thought I saw a wisp of moisture, it turned out to be a trick of the eye, sunlight glancing off dust.

I wondered what our father was doing right now. Had he gone to the army to report our disappearance? Had he told our mother?

In her fragile state, the news could make her worse. But surely she would notice our absence. The more I thought about it, the more I became sick with anxiety—not for myself, but for my parents. In the front of the truck, I felt strangely secure with Ulysses driving, although I knew I should be frightened. But when I thought of my parents—alone and worried—I was seized with panic. I reached for Will's hand, and though he was pretending to be asleep against the door, he twined his fingers with mine and held tight.

We spent the night in the truck with the dogs. Ulysses said it was too dangerous to sleep in the tents. I didn't think pirates were afraid of anything, but he explained that Minnesota was one of the few places where wild animals still roamed freely. They were aggressive and hungry and would think nothing of eating a couple of children if they could. Although it was cold in the truck and grew colder as the night deepened, Ulysses had plenty of blankets. In the darkest part of the night, he started the engine and warmed the truck with the heater. The rumble of the engine and the warm circulating air soon made me drowsy, and I fell back asleep.

In the morning I awoke with my head against Ulysses's shoulder. For a moment, before I was fully awake, I could swear he was watching me. But when I opened my eyes, he was looking straight ahead.

"Where are we going?" I asked, rubbing my forehead with the palm of one hand. I was embarrassed to have fallen asleep on him and didn't want him to think I had noticed.

"You'll know when we get there," said the pirate.

"How do *you* know where you're going?" I asked.

"A pirate's intuition," said Ulysses. When he smiled the creases around his mouth looked like deep crags. He shook off his blankets and opened the door of the truck. "You stay here," he commanded.

I watched him walk to the closest truck, his broad shoulders swaying as if he were carrying a weight, one leg dragging slightly, the dogs at his side. He had told us pirates didn't fight except when forced to; they preferred to use stealth and cunning. But most of the pirates I had seen were crossed with scars, missing fingers, and crooked or bent limbs. For men who didn't like to fight, they were well-bruised and battle-worn.

"They're taking us farther north," I said.

"I know," said Will.

"Why are they following Kai?"

"We don't know it's Kai. It could be any boy and his father."

"If they're following him, it means he's still alive."

Will nodded.

"But if he's alive and they learn that we know him, then we're in danger," I whispered.

"We're already in danger."

"Why can't the army rescue us?" By now the RGs had surely reviewed the security logs and would be looking for us. I would gladly take being arrested over being killed.

Will shook his head. "They won't cross the border. You know that."

The lower republics would not risk war with Minnesota over two missing children—not when they were already at war with the Empire of Canada and the Arctic Archipelago. Although Minnesota was technically neutral, the republics depended on it for fresh water. They would do nothing to upset that delicate balance. By crossing the border, we had lost all hope of rescue.

We stared out the front window, watching the pirates gathering inside the circle of trucks. Someone had made a fire, and breakfast was cooking. The salty, smoky smell of something frying in a pan drifted into the front cab. My stomach grumbled. I realized I had not eaten since breakfast the day before. I was famished. Will, too, sniffed eagerly.

Ulysses gestured for us to get out of the truck. I hesitated until he made an eating motion: cupping one hand and putting it to his mouth. Then I scrambled from the seat and jumped to the ground. Will followed.

"Hungry?" Ulysses asked when I reached him.

I didn't wait for a second question. I took the first plate offered.

The food was delicious. Ulysses said it was real bacon, grown on a real farm. I had never eaten real bacon before and licked my plate clean. Growing animals was expensive and dangerous, and it was only permitted by government license. It was a waste of resources, the government said, water that could be put to better use. Yet somehow WABs managed to provide meat at their own tables.

I noticed the bald pirate who had first spoken to us in the truck. His name was Ali, and he called out to me as I passed with a plate of seconds. He wore a kev-jacket and a long scarf loosely wrapped around his neck. When I approached he smiled widely. "Not so frightened anymore, are we, missy?" he asked.

It was true that I found him friendly and even humorous, but I couldn't help thinking the pirates were taking us away from our parents to a place from which we might not return. The pirates were nice to us now, but Will and I were still prisoners, not free to leave or go our own way. I waved to him and moved on.

The pirates spent the rest of the morning preparing the trucks, unloading and reloading materials. They were skilled mechanics; small clusters of men worked under the chassis or on the engines. Gasoline-powered vehicles were rare and temperamental, although they could out-haul anything electric. In a pinch, they could be rigged to burn siphoned bio-gas from a generator while the electrical grid was unreliable and often unavailable. This was why our father had bought our pedicycles which, I remembered sadly, were now abandoned hundreds of kilometers behind us on the road.

The way the pirates squeezed their supplies into the trucks was like a feat of magic. Not only were there weapons and explosives, but cans of food, fabric, blankets, clothing, shoes, electrical parts, tools, spare tires, oxygen, medicine, carbon blocks, nails, salt, chlorine, and iodine. There were even boxes of real beer which Ulysses would not let us near because, he claimed, it was worth more than everything else combined. In short they had all they needed for a prolonged journey or extended siege. "Be prepared," said Ulysses. "That's our motto."

It seemed to be a silly motto, but Ulysses looked deadly serious as he hauled boxes into the back of the truck. The sweat shone on his brow despite the morning chill, and muscles flexed beneath his shirt. I tried to lift a box to help, but it was too heavy, so I occupied myself by gathering the small things the pirates had overlooked.

Cheetah followed me everywhere I went, and I quickly learned to distinguish her from her sister, because Cheetah's fur had flecks of black mixed in with the gold, she was smaller than Pooch, and her left ear flopped to one side. She even let me pet her and growled contentedly. It was hard to believe this was the same animal that had pursued us on the road, and it made me wonder whether I had been wrong to fear her at all.

Will wandered off to watch two pirates repair an axle, and before long he was scampering beneath the wheels and following their directions.

By noon the trucks were reorganized in an arrangement known only to the pirates. Nothing looked different, yet everything was in a new place. Ulysses gave the signal, and the men climbed into their vehicles. Will joined me in the front seat of the truck. Cheetah and Pooch squeezed into the small compartment behind us.

"The men are getting ready for a battle," said Will.

"How do you know?"

"They told me."

I didn't believe it, although Will seemed sure. When I asked Ulysses, he just grunted. "Pirates are always prepared for battle," he said. He wouldn't say anything more.

"Didn't you notice?" said Will. "Their tankers are empty. They're going to steal what they can't buy."

"Pirates don't steal," said Ulysses. "We make offers people can't refuse."

"What does that mean?" I asked.

"It means they steal," said Will.

Ulysses smiled.

If there was going to be a battle, I didn't want to be in the middle of it. The Minnesotans—or whomever the pirates were meeting—would not give up their water without a fight. Although I didn't understand the politics, I was certain the pirates couldn't just drive into a republic, pay off the border guards, steal water, and drive out again. But that's exactly what it appeared they were doing.

And what did it all have to do with Kai? If they were following him with empty tankers, he must be somewhere near water—maybe even the secret river. But that meant he was in the hands of the Minnesotans, which didn't make much sense. Surely the Minnesotans didn't need another driller; they got enough water from the Canadians and still had access to underground lakes. Crossing the border to kidnap two people was an international violation and an act of war. I couldn't imagine why the Minnesotans would take that risk. Suddenly I was very scared.

I found Will's hand and gripped it tightly. He squeezed back, and for a while that was all I needed.

By late afternoon the landscape had changed. Where there had been dust, dirt, and debris, there were now the faintest signs of civilization: a concrete bunker with smoke rising from a chimney; an electric car that wasn't rusted or broken; roads that were nearly smooth; and the most telling sign of all—patches of green.

"*They're growing,*" said Will, his voice hushed and awestruck.

Except for photos of Basin and the occasional hardy plant or backyard scrub, we rarely saw anything green that wasn't painted on or in a hydro-vault. But here it looked as if people had water to spare. Green things sprouted up in no particular pattern, almost as if no one cared where they grew.

"It's grass," Ulysses explained. "They feed it to the cattle."

"They have cattle?" Will asked in a whisper.

"How do you think they get meat?"

"But…" Will's voice trailed off. Such riches were unimaginable. Flowing water, grass, and cattle—it was as if someone said that gold paved the streets and diamonds were in the hills.

Then in the distance, I saw our destination. It loomed in front of us like a gigantic wall that stretched the length of an entire city. It was perfectly flat, yet seemingly endless, with nothing rising behind it, as if no one dared peer over the top. I had never seen such a thing, but I knew from the wireless that it was a giant dam holding back billions of liters of fresh water—water that might normally have flowed south to the border and maybe even to our home. Minnesota was the land of ten thousand dams, and its government often boasted that it had more dams per person than any other country in the world. I knew that the largest dam in the world was in the Arctic Straits, owned by Canada but claimed by the Arctic Archipelago. Someday, if the war ever ended, whoever controlled it would control ten percent of the world's fresh water.

Gray cliffs rose at either end of the dam—the same color as the concrete that had been used to build it. As Ulysses drove closer, I could see a small army of trucks and equipment parked around the dam's base, painted in the familiar blue-green of the Minnesota flag.

What were the pirates doing? Were they planning to steal water from the reservoir? Such a brazen act would get us all killed. The dam was heavily fortified, with gun batteries spaced regularly along its walls and the Minnesota Water Guard standing watch all across its length. There would be no escape, and stealing water was a capital crime.

I must have been fidgeting on the seat, because Ulysses turned to me and said, "Don't fret, little sister. We're just here for talking. Even pirates know their limits."

"Is this where they've taken the boy?" I asked. "The one you're following?"

Will pinched my thigh, but I ignored him. I gave Ulysses my most innocent look, as if my interest were purely theoretical.

"Taken? What makes you think they've taken him?"

I tried to keep my voice steady. "Isn't that what you said?"

"We don't know he's been taken. But we know they've been here."

"Were they drilling in Minnesota?" I asked.

To drill for another republic was treason, which might explain why Kai and his father disappeared so quickly and why the RGs were looking for them. It still didn't explain the pirates' interest, but if Kai's father had discovered a secret river, the pirates would want the water for themselves. If pirates wanted what the Minnesotans had, there would be a fight. And here we were, traveling with Ulysses right into the heart of it.

"Not drilling," said Ulysses. "Planning." I didn't say anything, but Ulysses kept talking. "There's a hydrologist works out of the research center—Dr. Tinker. Older guy, looks like Albert Einstein. He gives them information, and they do the same."

"But he's a Minnesotan," I said.

"It's people who draw these boundaries," said Ulysses. "The earth and sky don't have borders."

"Maybe. But the Minnesotans think they do."

"As I said, we're just talking. Convincing comes later."

Ulysses might have said more, but the flash came first, followed by the sound. It was as if lightning struck three times in quick succession, except the sky was clear, and thunderstorms were a thing of fiction and holo-casts. Then the concussive booms followed, each one more violent than the last.

What happened next was unlike anything I had ever seen or was likely to see again. The middle section of the great dam began to collapse. It happened in slow motion: the walls trembled and seemed to melt inward, then a fissure opened in the middle into which each end was gradually swallowed.

Water, billions and billions of liters, rushed over the top of the broken wall and into the valley below. It spilled from the great dam, sweeping trucks, concrete, and people before it. It came down from the cliffs and rushed toward us, as fast and furious as a tidal wave or an earthquake—an unleashed, angry river, the power of which was something no person could control.

We didn't even have time to run.

CHAPTER 9

The first thing I noticed when I awoke was that my clothes were soaking wet and plastered to my body. I had never been wet without a mask, and never when fully dressed. It was a huge waste of water, potentially dangerous and likely to make me sick. These were the lessons I had learned in the classroom, at a desk in a school that was now hundreds of kilometers away.

I tried to move, but my sides ached painfully. One leg was bent behind me as if it belonged to someone else. My hands were scratched and bleeding, and I could taste more blood in my mouth. I felt for teeth and was relieved to find they appeared to be intact. I pressed against them with my tongue, confirming that none were loose or broken. I managed to lift my head a few centimeters from the ground, but I could only see mud, rocks, and water. I could also hear a rushing sound, like a steady wind blowing through sand. But there was no wind and no sand. My head sank back into the mud.

It came back to me then. The explosions. The dam collapsing. Ulysses throwing open the doors and pushing us from the truck. After that everything was a blur. The waters caught me and swept me away. It was like the ancient river our father had described—so much water rushing wildly over everything in its path. I struggled to stay afloat, then just let myself be taken wherever the river intended.

Time passed. I didn't know how much. It might have been an hour; it might have been a day. Although I felt dizzy and was in pain, I was able to pull my leg beneath me and, by propping myself up with my elbows, move into a sitting position. From there I could see the ruined landscape, the chunks of concrete and metal. Water ran everywhere, and even the skies were dark and muddied. There was no sign of the dam or of the people and machines, although I could still see the cliffs where the structure had once been seamlessly joined. No Will. No Ulysses. Everything had been swept away.

I realized how hungry I was, and despite being soaked, how thirsty. I cupped my hands to sip some water from the pool in front of me. In school the teachers had drilled it into us not to drink anything that didn't have a government stamp on it, but I couldn't remember the last time I'd drunk. The water might make me sick, but what choice did I have? I leaned over and scooped the liquid into my hands.

The water was delicious—cool, fresh, and invigorating. It tasted like the water Kai had brought with him to dinner at our home: real water, unfiltered and without chemicals, straight from the sky into a river, from which it flowed up to the dam. I scooped up several more handfuls, drinking my fill until my belly hurt, and I burped loudly.

I sat straighter and looked around again. I guessed it was the middle of the afternoon. Though it was warmer than normal for the time of year, within a few hours, it would soon grow cold. I knew I couldn't survive the night outside in wet clothes. Already I felt chilled to the bone, and my fingers were numb. If I didn't start moving, I might perish just from sitting still. I placed my palms on the ground and pushed myself unsteadily to my feet. I swayed woozily in the thick air until my balance returned. Then I began to walk.

At first I followed the river downstream. It seemed natural to follow the flow of water, which rippled and coiled like a living thing. But as my head cleared, I realized the chances of finding survivors were greater back at the dam. There was more likely to be food and shelter there too. So I turned, retraced my steps, and made my way upriver.

With each step my feet squeaked. The water had soaked through my shoes, and my toes rubbed against hard plastene. I had barely walked a kilometer before my skin was raw. Another kilometer, and my toes were bloody. I gritted my teeth and forced myself to go on. Step, step, step. I counted each one. As I got closer to the dam, I saw a pile of clothes abandoned by the side of the river, but when I approached, I realized it was actually a dead body twisted in a gruesome way. I covered my eyes and moved quickly ahead. However, the dead bodies were everywhere. Their faces were bloated, and their limbs were discolored and swollen. It was hard to believe that water could kill so many people, but the proof was right there in front of me. Perhaps the people caught by the river could not believe it either until the water had swept them away.

I tried hard not to think about Will, but I couldn't help looking at each body, praying that none was him. Ulysses had pushed us both from the truck, and Will had grabbed my hand. But the river separated us immediately, plunging us down into the watery depths from which I emerged alone. If Will was out there, he had surfaced somewhere else. I had to believe he was looking for me as I was looking for him. I refused to accept any other truth but that he had managed to survive somehow. It was my only hope, and it kept me moving. Each step might bring us closer.

Then I saw something that made my heart hammer in my chest: a familiar jacket and a long scarf. It was Ali, the pirate who had sat with us in the back of the truck. His mouth was open in an expression of surprise, as if he had tried to drink the water before it killed him. Nearby I recognized another pirate, and then another. Altogether there were six of them grouped closely, soaked and exposed, tattoos blending with purplish bruises and swollen skin. Their bulletproof clothing had not saved them from drowning. In fact, the weight had dragged them under. But I was relieved to discover Ulysses was not among them, nor could I see the dogs, Cheetah and Pooch. I averted my eyes and walked swiftly away.

It was growing dark. Nothing moved except the water. It appeared to be endless, still flowing out of the dam, running downstream toward who knew where. My teeth throbbed, and the skin on my hands was shriveled and yellowed. I sat on the wet ground. This time I couldn't control the sobs. They consumed me, wracking my chest, crushing the air from my lungs. I was alone, truly alone. I was cold, hungry, and wet, and in a matter of hours, it would be too dark to see. Nothing but ruin surrounded me in every direction.

There was no place for shelter, no safety. My brother was missing; Kai was gone; the pirates were dead; and all was lost. I cried until I could cry no more, and my head pounded in agony.

Then in the distance, I saw a light. It swept across the landscape, probing and inquisitive. It shot high into the sky, then swept low across the land. I stood and waved, summoning it to draw close. I didn't care about the danger or who might be near. Nothing could be worse than staying out all night alone in the soaked and broken land. A light meant people, and people would mean food, water, dry clothes. I jumped up, trying to catch the beams with my hands. But the light danced and shimmied, never resting in any one place for long. Several times it arced above my head, then fell short just before my feet. It seemed to have a mind of its own, sniffing out the corners of the earth in search of something only it knew. Then for several minutes it disappeared entirely, and I thought I was doomed. But it reemerged in a different position— closer and more intense. I broke into a run, trying to capture it before it disappeared again.

I heard the men, then—loud voices shouting and the crackling of radios. I heard something else too that made me stop in my tracks: gunfire. Short staccato bursts. I had never heard gunfire before, but it was unmistakable. Each bullet was clear, crisp, and final. A string of them together sounded like balloons popping in a frenzied burst. I turned to run, but it was too late; the light caught me, and I was frozen in its glare.

Two gloved hands grabbed me and threw me roughly to the ground. I didn't even try to fight; I just lay there, silently waiting for the end. Then the light was upon me, so bright I couldn't even open my eyes. I heard a voice, but I couldn't understand the words. *Kee-ay-too*, the voice said. *Kee-ay-too?*

It's French, I thought. The men were Canadian. Had the truce between Minnesota and Canada been broken? Were the countries at war? The world was too large and complex to grasp. The intricate allegiances of governments and people seemed to flutter as unpredictability as that butterfly in the jet stream. I was just a girl trying to find my brother, my friend, and my way home.

Then in perfect English, the voice said, "Who are you?"

I opened my eyes, but I still could not see.

"Who are you?" the voice repeated again.

"Vera," I said.

"How did you get here?"

"The pirates brought me."

"Shut off the damned light," said the voice.

The world was plunged back into night. Now I could see the man standing over me. He wore a green beret, a dark green shirt, and green camouflage pants. The men surrounding him were dressed similarly. I assumed they were wearing the uniform of the Canadian army, or maybe the Water Guard. Will would know if he were here. I fought back another round of tears.

"Who are *you?*" I asked.

"The People's Environmental Liberation Army," the man said proudly.

I had heard of PELA but thought the organization was just a horror story told by shakers to frighten kids. PELA did terrible things—bombing desalinization plants, poisoning reservoirs, kidnapping and killing WAB ministers, burning oil supplies. They made pirates look like respectable citizens. Now I was in their hands.

"Did you blow up the dam?"

"Of course we blew up the dam," said the man. He seemed offended that I might think otherwise.

"And kill all those pirates?"

"Most definitely."

"And what about the Minnesotans?"

"They're dead too."

I took in all this information. It was almost too much to bear. My father once told us that all people believed in the same God, although each had a different name for Him. But Will said there was no God, just a need for people to believe. Wherever they were, I hoped Ali and the pirates were at peace.

"Are you the leader?" I asked.

"I'm Nasri," said the man. "Chief environmental scientist."

"You're not much of a scientist."

"Who do you think invented those explosives? Ordinary dynamite or C4 couldn't blow such a structure."

Nasri was practically hopping on one foot, as if he couldn't wait to get going in some race. He was small and wiry with a short beard and stubbly hair. Once I got a good look at him, he didn't frighten me at all, although his eyes looked wild—one brown, one blue—and I could see them shining even in the darkness. His men hung back, as if they didn't know whom he might strike next. There were eight of them, each bearded, each wearing the same combat outfit.

"They'll come after you," I said. "Now that they know you've blown the dam."

"You're an expert?" asked Nasri. "It's twenty-five kilometers to Canada, and there's clear passage all the way to Niagara."

Canada? Were Nasri and his men allied with the Canadians? If so it was a strange alliance. The Canadians had destroyed the environment, hoarding much of Earth's water and killing thousands of species of fish and land animals. Years ago their prime minister had been indicted for environmental crimes by the world court, although he was never prosecuted after the court was destroyed in a terrorist attack and the chief justice was killed.

"Shouldn't be surprised," said Nasri. "The Canadians need us, and we need the Canadians. Suits all our purposes."

"But what about when the war is over?"

Nasri laughed—a short, sharp bark. "The war will never be over. Not as long as there's water on Earth. Humans will fight for the last drop."

"I don't believe it. Earth is too important."

"Ha! You're an environmentalist."

"If being an environmentalist means blowing things up and killing people, I'd rather be a pirate."

Nasri stopped hopping and fixed me with a glare. "No one's giving you a choice. Now get moving." He pushed me hard toward his men.

"I can't walk anymore. I think my toes are broken."

Nasri signaled with one open hand, and a hover-carrier appeared as if from nowhere, pulling up beside him and floating silently. I had never seen a hover-carrier before. They were very expensive, owned only by the military and the wealthiest WABs. Fast, sleek, and silent, a hover-carrier could reach speeds of 250 kilometers an hour without kicking up any dust as it glided over the rocks and dirt. I couldn't imagine how PELA could afford one, but before I could even ponder that riddle, two more hover-carriers glided to a halt beside the first. Men in camouflage jumped from the back and stood at attention, waiting for Nasri's orders.

"Search the bodies," he said. "Take any weapons you find and all their personal effects. We'll ransom them back to the families."

The men broke into groups and fanned out downriver. Nasri turned his attention to me. "Into the carrier," he ordered.

"Where are you taking me?"

"You may still be valuable. Do you have all your teeth?" He fingered my mouth. I winced and pulled away.

"The army knows we're here."

"In Minnesota?"

"We're from Minnesota."

Nasri smiled. His teeth were small and flat, worn down like a desert rat's. "Not likely," he said. "Now get into the truck."

He shoved me roughly toward the hover-carrier. Another man grabbed my arm and yanked so hard that I practically fell into the back of the cargo hold. I stumbled, then regained my balance, but the man had already slammed the door shut behind me. I grabbed the handle. It would not open, and the glass was thick and obviously bulletproof. I pounded at it with my palms, but it barely made a sound. My nails hurt just trying to scratch it.

I turned, and my eyes adjusted to the dark. I picked out boxes, weapons, and electronic equipment lining the shelves in the narrow hold. Many things were still wrapped, untouched, as if they had been newly purchased. There seemed to be no order, just rows of expensive items—loot from PELA operations. On the far wall I noticed a small machine with the name *Bluewater* stamped on it, which I assumed was the owner or manufacturer of the machine.

Then I noticed something else as well—a body lying prone on the ground. A boy's body. He was bloody and covered with mud. He didn't move.

"Will!" I cried.

CHAPTER 10

The hover-carriers glided silently over the ravaged land. Where rivers once flowed, there were now only huge gashes like scars on the earth. Lake beds had dried up, forming dust bowls that swirled with toxic chemicals and heavy metals. The ice and permafrost that covered the northern reaches had disappeared or been melted for water. The sea levels had risen, and salt water poisoned any underground aquifers that were not depleted from years of overuse. Rain fell, but in such torrents and violent storms that most of it washed into the ocean. The weather was unpredictable, and humans stole the clouds, sucking moisture from the sky and using it for their own purposes. Drought and death darkened the continents, and even the fittest could barely survive.

Nasri told me these things while my brother lay cradled in my lap. Will's face was hot with fever and damp with perspiration, but at least he was alive. I brushed the hair from his eyes and kissed him lightly on the forehead. He stirred but did not speak. Nasri had given him some medicine, but it didn't seem to be working. His leg was infected and raw, and it would take more than pills to cure it.

"We have to get him to a doctor," I said.

"He'll live," said Nasri.

"You don't know that."

"I have seen men with legs seeping maggots survive in the desert. Their legs were simply amputated, and they moved on."

"You can't amputate his leg!"

Nasri shrugged. "We do what we have to. This is war."

"We're not fighting your war."

"Of course you are. We're all fighting the war."

"What war are you fighting?" I demanded.

"We're fighting on the side of the land."

"The land? By blowing up dams and sabotaging water supplies? By killing anyone who crosses your path? You talk about saving the land, but you're poisoning it."

Nasri blinked rapidly. He looked like he wanted to hop again, but there was no room to hop in the small cargo hold.

"We're poisoning the land to save it," he spat. "When the great dams and reservoirs are destroyed, the water will return to the land, and people will remember its precious gift."

"That's crazy."

Nasri raised his hand, and I flinched, but he merely scratched his stubbly head. "Look after your brother," he said. Then he opened the hatch to the carrier's main compartment and disappeared into the front of the truck.

I sat in the darkness and listened to Will breathe. I would not let him lose his leg. I would find him a doctor—a real doctor—who would give him proper medicine and stitch it up. And what of Kai? Was he already dead? The seriousness of our predicament was not lost on me. We were now in Canada, a country with which we were at war. We had no travel papers and were dependent on the kindness of environmental mercenaries—lowlife thugs who couldn't be trusted. There was something suspicious about PELA's avowed alliance with the Canadians—the very people who had dammed Earth's water and melted the giant icebergs. I lay down next to Will, gripping his hand with my fingers. I could feel the pulse in his wrist, strong and steady. Will was a fighter. As long as his heart kept beating, he would not give up. I remembered how he pumped for both of us on the pedicycle, pushing past the point of exhaustion. It seemed like another lifetime ago. The dusty road where I had witnessed a boy spilling water from a cup was as far away as the girl I had once been—a girl who had never heard gunfire or seen a man swollen and dead.

I fell into a restless sleep. In my dreams, my parents and Will were gliding down a giant river on a floating device that looked like a pedicycle with its wheels turned sideways. I tried to warn them they were not safe. Water was leaking in through the wheels and swamping their seats. They were pedaling while slowly sinking. But they just waved happily back at me, oblivious to the danger. The river moved swiftly and silently, torrents of water rushing to the ocean. Dark and violent, it swirled around them like a gathering storm. I watched helplessly from the muddy shoreline as my family was swept away into the unforgiving sea.

I awoke to find Will still lying next to me. It took a moment to realize that he had one eye open and was staring at me, just as he used to do back home when we pulled our mattresses together in my room.

"Vera," he whispered.

"Will!"

"Where are we?"

I explained we were in the back of a hover-carrier, traveling with PELA along the Canadian border.

"PELA?" he croaked.

"They blew up the dam," I said. "It wiped out everything. Ulysses and the pirates are dead."

Will shut his one open eye as if trying to block the loss, but when he opened both eyes, all he said was, "My leg hurts." He reached down to pull up his trouser leg. His skin was red and raw, and blood and yellow fluid oozed down his calf. But a scab had begun to form around the edges, and purplish bruising mottled his shin.

"They gave you some medicine," I said.

"Why would they do that?"

"They want to sell us."

Healthy children of working age were needed at the drilling sites, Nasri had said. They were small enough to scramble down the narrow shafts but took in one-tenth the pay of adults. Plenty of orphans were apprenticed to the mines, their lives as miserable as the nineteenth-century urchins we'd learned about in school. As far as PELA was concerned, we were orphans they had found on the road.

"But we have parents!" protested Will.

"They don't care. They just want money."

"Maybe PELA kidnapped Kai."

I had considered this. Several years ago three brothers were kidnapped from a Skate 'n' Sand arena. They never returned, although rumors circulated that they were working for a drilling company on the Great Coast. This was why our father insisted that we shouldn't talk to strangers and that we wi-text him when we were leaving school. But I didn't think PELA had taken Kai. The environmentalists couldn't have come into town without drawing notice, and it was too far south for them to venture anyway. PELA operated on the borders, near reservoirs and dams, where they could strike quickly then retreat.

"Wherever he is," I said, "we've got to find him."

"We've got to get out of here is what we've got to do."

"Not without Kai."

Will sat up on one elbow and drew his good leg beneath him. "Listen, Vera. We don't know where he is, or who took him, or even if he's gone. It was stupid to go chasing after him in the first place. Now if we don't get out of here, the environmentalists are going to sell us—or worse."

I blushed, feeling chastened by my brother's words. But I refused to be cowed into agreement. "The pirates know where he is."

"They're dead. You said so yourself."

"We don't know for sure. Some are dead, but some may have survived."

Will was a fighter. He would never give up—not when there was still a chance. He would lead his troops into battle and fight to his last breath. That's why I couldn't believe it when he said, "It's hopeless."

"What do you mean?"

"We're in Canada, Vera. We're prisoners in the country of our enemies. Even if we could find Kai, we can't save him. How could we? Be realistic. We're just two kids without any weapons, and we'll be lucky to get out of here with our own lives."

"No, Will. Don't say that!"

"It's true. Look at me. My leg is infected. I need a doctor. Our parents probably think we're dead. We have to forget about Kai and the river. We have to get home!"

When other kids couldn't raise another bucket, Will kept lifting. When they thought the condensers were emptied, Will found the last drop. He was always the first to volunteer and the last to leave. Yes, he was injured, and our situation was desperate, but we were not so far gone that all hope was lost.

"Kai is our friend," I said. "You can try to get home—if you want—but I'm going to stay here until I find him."

"Don't be ridiculous. We're locked in the back of a truck."

"I don't care! I'm going to get out." I walked to the rear doors of the carrier and banged on the handles as hard as I could. They wouldn't budge. Even if I could force the doors open, the carrier was traveling at hundreds of kilometers an hour, and the fall to the ground would surely kill me. But the only thing that mattered right then was getting out. I tried prying at the bars that covered two small windows on each side of the truck, but the metal was cold and unyielding. I stamped my feet on the floor as hard as I could.

"Open the doors!" I shouted. It made me angry that people could simply kill other people, take what they wanted, and ignore the cries of the sick and hungry. The world wasn't like that—or it shouldn't be like that—even though I hadn't seen enough of the world to know what it was really like. I pounded at the fortified steel until my wrists felt like breaking. "Open the doors!" I shouted again. "This is wrong! You are wrong! Open the doors!"

Suddenly Will was beside me, leaning on my shoulder for support. "Stop, Vera. Stop. I'll help you."

I looked at my brother, and I could see how much it pained him to stand. But he stood; and though his face was pale, his grip was strong. "I'll help you," he said again.

"You're hurt."

"It's not that bad."

"Do you really think we can get out of here?"

"I do."

If we were going to escape, however, we would have to wait until the environmentalists stopped to refuel or sleep. Anything else would mean certain death. So while the carrier raced eastward, we searched the cargo hold. Shiny electronics, unwrapped and gleaming, lined the shelves. Dried food in airtight boxes and water in sealed containers were crammed in next to them. Although there were dozens of weapons, we couldn't find any ammunition or fuses for the grenades. I didn't see any of the explosives used to blow up the dam, but I figured they had either been detonated or stored in another carrier. Nasri was smart enough to keep them out of our hands. Finally we came upon the Bluewater machine.

"Where do you think they got this?" asked Will.

"Probably stole it, like everything else."

"It's worth a lot of money. Not too many of these around."

"What is it?"

"A portable desalinator."

Desalinization was an expensive and complicated process in which salt and minerals were removed from water to make it drinkable. Most desalinization plants were on the ocean, where they spit their waste back into the sea, killing fish and marine life but producing plenty of water. A portable desalinator, however, would let its owner travel almost anywhere and not worry about dying of thirst. The dirtiest, saltiest puddle could be made to produce clean, drinkable water. "Help me lift it," said Will.

"There's plenty of water," I said and pointed to the sealed crates.

"I don't want to make more water."

"What do you want to do, then?"

"Just help me."

The desalinator was heavier than it looked. We tried to lift it, but Will could barely hold on. Every time we got it more than a few centimeters off the ground, Will's leg hurt too much to hold it. Finally we half-dragged, half-carried it over to the rear doors. Will was grimacing in pain by the time we finished.

"Your leg," I said.

We both looked down at Will's calf. It had begun to bleed again, a bright red color that was different from the oozing yellow pus.

"It's fine," said Will, although it wasn't. He sat on the floor and began to tinker with the machine. First he lifted the cover and peered inside. Then he pulled out one wire, and a second. Soon he had half the top open.

"This thing kicks off a ton of heat," said Will. "It's how they desalinate water. Flash boiling, and then condensation."

"We don't need to condense water."

"But we might want to boil it."

I could almost see the plan forming in Will's brain. He had the same look as when he was about to pounce with a pillow. Equal parts mischief and determination. I knew not to ask questions.

Will handed me a hose he had yanked from the inside of the machine. "Hold this," he said.

I followed his instructions while he sorted, crimped, and twisted. More than once Will had repaired the school's condensers before the maintenance crews could arrive. Now he worked like a boy possessed, removing tubes and hoses and reattaching them in different places. His face was feverish, but his hands were steady, and if his leg hurt, he didn't show it. He chewed on his lip, squinted liberally, and, when he was momentarily stuck, rubbed his forehead like a lamp for good luck. Finally he stepped back to admire his invention.

"Now we need some ammunition," he said.

By now I had a pretty good idea of Will's intentions. I handed him a canister of pure water from one of the shelves, and he poured it into the machine. We would be ready when the environmentalists stopped—if they stopped.

"Where do you think they're going?" I asked.

Will shrugged. Like the pirates, PELA operated freely among the republics and Canada. They were outlaws too, but with better public relations and more powerful friends.

"Why do you think they came to Minnesota in the first place?" he asked.

"To blow the dam."

Will shook his head. "Too small. And there's another dam downstream. It'll catch all the water."

I had stopped asking how Will knew all these things; he just knew facts most kids did not. As large as the dam looked, Will was correct it was smaller than average. Yet there were a million reasons PELA might have blown it—most of them unknowable except to the guerillas themselves. Will, however, already had some ideas.

"Let's say they were at the dam for another reason."

"Such as?"

We sat next to each other with a box of semiautomatic pistols as our backrest. Will lifted his leg and rested it on my shin to keep it elevated, and the warmth and weight of it calmed me. It was almost like being at home, talking late past our bedtimes until our father caught us and pretended to be angry.

"Maybe there was a person both the pirates and PELA wanted to visit," Will said.

"Dr. Tinker?"

Will nodded slowly. "Environmentalists don't care much for water explorers."

"But why would they blow the dam?"

Will wrinkled his nose, but before he could respond, the hovercarrier slowed, then came to a gentle rest on something firm. I could hear the crunch of earth and rock. I looked at Will, and he signaled for me to be quiet. He stood, and with my help he inched the desalinator closer to the door. His leg was bleeding again, but he didn't notice. Instead he flipped a switch on the machine and took a hose in his hand. The machine started humming quietly and gave off a smell like two rocks cracked together. Will and I crouched in the darkness, silent except for the sound of our breathing. We stood for what seemed like an hour. I thought my legs would give out. My toes ached, and the scratches in my hands were inflamed. I couldn't imagine what Will must be feeling. The pain was nearly unearthly.

Then outside we heard men talking.

"They don't care about the doctor," said a man's voice.

"And the children?"

"It's good money for the mines."

"Shame."

"Not our problem."

Someone fiddled with the locks, and then the door creaked open. Sunlight streamed into the cargo hold like a bouquet of sharp needles. A man stepped into the doorway, blocking the sun. It took him a moment to adjust to the darkness, and in that space, quick as a sand fly, Will sprang.

The man screamed and fell backward into the dirt.

CHAPTER 11

Run, Will, run!" I screamed.

Will stood in the open doorway of the cargo hold, shooting hot steam over the prone bodies of two guards. It was as if he were frozen, unable to move. Then he snapped out of it and let me help him out of the truck.

"Quick, they'll be here in a second," I said.

"I can't run."

"I'll help you."

Will shook his head. "The carrier. We can drive it."

"I don't know how to drive."

"I do," he insisted.

Even if Will could drive with his injured leg, there was a big difference between steering a rundown electric car and a hydrogen-fueled hovercraft capable of going several hundred kilometers an hour. On the other hand, I knew it was our only real chance. If we evaded the environmentalists, we still wouldn't get far on the sand. The carrier gave us a fighting chance of escape. As for the border, we would just have to deal with it when we reached it. *If* we reached it.

I helped Will limp to the front of the carrier, averting my eyes from the burned bodies of the two guards by the rear door. There were three other carriers about two hundred meters distant, and men hustled about, unloading supplies and equipment. No one had noticed us yet, but our absence wouldn't go undetected for long.

Will pulled himself into the driver's seat, and I swung around to the other side of the front cab. The instrument panel was complicated, packed with levers and switches. There was no steering wheel; just two paddles thick with buttons. It didn't look anything like our father's car. Will flipped a switch on the front panel, but nothing happened; then he pushed another one, and the panel lit up.

"You sure you know what you're doing?" I asked.

"I know," said Will, sounding annoyed.

"They could shoot us."

"Not if they want their desalinator."

Will was right. If PELA destroyed the carrier, they would destroy the desalinator and all the weapons in the hold. They might be able to replace the weapons, but a portable desalinator was extremely rare and would literally keep them alive. Nasri and his men would think twice before risking its loss. They didn't know, of course, that Will had already dismantled it.

The engine made a whirring noise that sounded promising. Then the carrier lurched forward a couple meters and stopped suddenly with a force that threw me to the floor.

"Sorry," said Will. "Buckle up."

I brushed myself off, and this time I buckled myself into the passenger seat. Will flipped a couple switches and gently squeezed both paddles. The hover-carrier lifted into the air, hovering about a meter above the ground.

"Now what?" I asked.

Will pulled back on one paddle while pushing the other forward, and the carrier rotated slowly in a circle. Then he reversed direction, and the carrier spun the other way. "Just like Death Racer," he said. When he brought the paddles back to the middle, the carrier stopped spinning and hovered above the ground. "Cool," he said.

Just then a man emerged from one of the other carriers. He was tall, with white hair that stood straight up, and he wore a scientist's white lab coat. Nasri followed closely behind him. The two men walked about ten meters, and then Nasri withdrew something from his pocket and waved it at the man.

"He's got a gun," I said.

The first man stopped, and Nasri walked two steps closer to him, leveling the gun at his back. The man turned, faced Nasri, and bowed his head toward the ground.

"It's Dr. Tinker," I said.

"I see him."

"They're going to kill him!"

Nasri stood before Dr. Tinker, his gun arm extended. I couldn't believe it, but it really did appear that Nasri was going to shoot the doctor in cold blood. "Will!" I shouted.

The hover-carrier bolted forward, pressing me back into my seat. Nasri looked up at the same time, momentarily perplexed by the carrier bearing down on him. He stumbled backward just as the carrier stopped. "Get him!" Will shouted to me.

Will had positioned us between Nasri and Dr. Tinker, with the rear cargo door facing the doctor. Through the front viewscreen I could see Nasri looking at us, his eyes turning into slits that promised violence. I knew I had only a handful of seconds before he acted.

I dashed to the back of the carrier and flung open the doors. Dr. Tinker was still looking down as if he expected to be shot. "Quick, into the truck!" I called. He looked up but didn't move, and I extended an arm. "Get in! Get in!"

He moved as if in a daze and grasped my hand as if unsure what he was holding. When he took his first steps into the carrier, I heard a pistol shot, and then Nasri appeared around the corner. He charged at me, raising his arm to fire a second shot. I shut my eyes. But the shot never came. Instead I heard Nasri scream, and I opened my eyes to see Will spraying him with hot steam from the desalinator. "The doors, Vera!"

I slammed the cargo doors shut while Will scrambled back into the driver's seat. We took off with a jolt that sent both Dr. Tinker and me to the floor. But I didn't mind. We weren't dead. In the bulletproof hover-carrier, moving at two hundred kilometers an hour, it would be difficult for Nasri to hurt us.

I helped Dr. Tinker into his seat. He let me fasten his buckle and adjust the headrest.

"Who are you?" he asked when I was seated.

"Who are *you?*" asked Will, turning slightly from the driver's seat.

"Doctor Augustus Tinker. Hydrologist."

"Pleased to meet you," I said. "I'm Vera. And this is my brother, Will."

Dr. Tinker looked at us as if I had just told him Will and I were Martians come down to perform experiments on his brain.

"We're not going to hurt you," I added.

The hover-carrier dipped suddenly in the air, and Dr. Tinker's head jerked forward then banged backward against the headrest.

"Sorry," said Will.

"My brother's never driven a hover-carrier," I explained.

"I'm doing a pretty good job." said Will sullenly. "Considering."

"But *who* are you?" Dr. Tinker repeated.

I told him our names again, and said we had been kidnapped by pirates, then by PELA, taken to Minnesota and then into Canada, and had escaped when Will rewired the portable desalinator. "We were trying to find Kai," I explained.

"Kai?"

"You know, the boy whose father works with you. The driller."

"Rikkai Smith?"

Will raised an eyebrow. "*Rikkai?*" he repeated.

"Tall, blond hair, about Will's age?" I asked.

The doctor nodded. "His father Driesen and I have been friends since before the Great Panic. But what made you think he was with me?"

"It's what the pirates said. They were coming to find you."

Dr. Tinker sniffed. "Instead those PELA thugs found me first."

I considered this. "What did they want from you?"

"The same thing the pirates wanted."

"Water," I said.

"Yes. Everyone wants water."

"But not everyone knows where to find it."

"Driesen has a special talent," said Tinker.

"Kai told us."

Dr. Tinker looked at me with a puzzled expression, as if he didn't understand what I had said. But his mouth was a thin, grim line, like a man who knew exactly what I meant. "What did he tell you?" he asked.

"A secret river with plenty of water, and no one has to get sick or fight anymore."

"Is it true?" asked Will.

But the doctor was silent and wouldn't say anything else. The hover-carrier sped over the ground, leaving the environmentalists behind. Will was getting the hang of driving now, and the ride was smooth and quick. Outside, the desert zipped past in a blur of sand and rock, with no green to be seen. Whatever water the Canadians owned, they had diverted it from this rocky and forlorn area.

"Do you have a plan to cross the border?" asked Dr. Tinker.

"Of course we do," I said. I looked at Will, wondering if he did. The hover-carrier was fast, but I doubted it could outrace border interceptors. For the first time, I also noted the fuel gauge was dangerously close to empty. This explained why the environmentalists had stopped before reaching their destination. But Will drove like it didn't matter.

"Those environmentalists were going to kill you," I said to Dr. Tinker.

"Yes," he said.

"You're lucky we found you."

"If we get across the border, I will see to it that you are adequately compensated."

"We'll get across," Will interjected.

Dr. Tinker did not sound like a man who was grateful his life had been saved. He seemed weary and slightly peeved, as if he had been interrupted in the middle of a game or favorite wi-cast.

"Did you work at the dam?" I asked.

"I worked at the laboratory powered by the dam." He explained that the research lab was in a different location than the turbines. It reduced the chances of sabotage.

"A lot of good that did," said Will.

The doctor nodded. "We knew it was vulnerable. But we thought security was adequate."

"Is that where you met Kai?" I asked.

"I've known Driesen for years, as I've explained."

"Were they visiting you?"

Dr. Tinker allowed himself a smile. He looked a little bit like a gnome, his hooked nose splitting his grin in half. "You'll not get any more information from me. These days even children are spies."

"Uh-oh," said Will. "Trouble."

"What?"

"We're out of fuel."

Indeed the carrier was slowing, and the ride was getting bumpier. One of the engines had quit, and the carrier listed to the right.

"Was this part of your plan too?" asked Dr. Tinker.

Will fought for control as we veered off the road. "Hold on," he said.

The carrier hit the ground with a bone-rattling thump. It threw me hard against the seat, then snapped my head back against the headrest. But it was nothing next to the earsplitting shriek as the carrier's bottom raked against the rocks.

"Wheels down, Will!" I shouted.

"They *are* down!"

We spun in a grinding arc, the shredding, screeching sound of metal against rock like a cacophonous symphony. Finally we came to a halt. There was a ragged gash where a side panel had been ripped open. Dust motes danced in the shards of sunlight that streamed through the gap.

"Well, I don't think we'll be doing much more driving," Dr. Tinker muttered.

Will looked at him sourly, then unbuckled his seat belt.

"Where do you think we can find some fuel?" I asked.

"I don't know!" Will snapped angrily. "What do I look like, a hydrogen diviner?"

"Now children," said Dr. Tinker.

Will slammed shut the carrier door, leaving me behind with Dr. Tinker.

"He's not really angry," I explained. "We've been through a lot."

"Remarkable. Did your parents recruit you?"

I wasn't going to waste breath trying to convince Dr. Tinker we weren't spies. He didn't intend to give us more information anyway, and I liked thinking of myself as a spy.

The door banged open, and Will jumped backed into the driver's seat. "They're coming!"

"Who?"

"PELA!"

Sure enough, through the cracked viewscreen I could see the dust kicked up from three hover-carriers about five kilometers down the road.

Will pressed the starting buttons on the instrument panel. The carrier's engine whined, but it failed to lift even a centimeter from the ground.

"We're doomed," said Dr. Tinker.

"What do we do?" I asked.

"You should have left me back there."

"Shut up!" said Will. He turned to me. "There's still a charge left in the desalinator."

I nodded and unbuckled my belt. I went to the back of the carrier while Will continued to try to start the engine. The desalinator's battery showed it had stored energy for perhaps two more bursts. It would not be enough to stop PELA, but if we could draw them outside, we might have a chance to steal another carrier.

After several more failed tries at the engine, Will joined me in the cargo hold. He took the hose from my hand, and we hunched near the doors.

"I wish we had bullets for the guns," I said.

"I don't want to kill anyone else."

"You had to kill those guards," I whispered.

Will carefully inspected the end of the hose, turning it over and over in his hands. "I'm sorry I yelled at you before."

"That's okay."

"I'm scared, Vera."

"So am I."

Will looked back up, and his eyes were red-rimmed and gray. I offered my brother my hand, and he grasped it like a last chance. "We're going to get home," I said. "Remember? You promised."

"I did," he said.

A concussive boom shook the carrier, knocking us both to the floor. It was followed by several smaller booms and then the sulfurous tang of torn metal.

"They're shooting at us!" I screamed. I was on the floor, my hands covering my head. Hot pieces of metal singed my hair and stung the backs of my arms.

"Stay down!" Will yelled.

Two more booms shattered the viewscreens inside the carrier. Glass rained onto the floor, and the cargo doors blew out. Small arms fire followed, the bullets ricocheting off the carrier's broken hulk. Smoke and dust swirled around the interior, making breathing nearly impossible. A single glass canister slipped from a shelf and smashed into a thousand pieces. I couldn't think, and I couldn't speak. All I could do was keep my head covered and pray it would end.

Then all fell silent. I raised my head. I was alive, and so was Will. I could not see Dr. Tinker.

A loudspeaker broke the silence.

"*Come out with your hands raised!*" said Nasri's amplified voice.

I looked over at Will and knew our situation was hopeless. Yet we lay there for several minutes until Nasri repeated himself and threatened to open fire again. Will raised his arms first, and I followed. We stepped over pieces of shredded metal and exited the carrier through a gaping hole where the driver's side door used to be. Dr. Tinker was already outside with his hands clasped above his head.

"If it isn't our little adventurers," said Nasri.

He smiled, but he was armed and angry. One side of his face looked burned and raw, and his neck was swathed in bandages. He hopped from one foot to the other. Even his men looked frightened. He waved his gun at the three of us and indicated we should move away from the carrier and stand out in the open.

"You're fools," he said. "No good will come of this."

"If you shoot us," I said, "you're throwing away good money."

Nasri raised his pistol. A shot rang out. When I opened my eyes, Dr. Tinker was dead on the ground.

CHAPTER 12

This time Nasri took no chances. He tied us up in the back of the carrier, then locked us to the door. He huffed, stomped, hopped, and grumbled about how he would make us pay for destroying the other carrier and his desalinator. He didn't seem to care at all for the men he'd lost, the man he had killed, or even his own injury—but the destruction of his machines was more than he could bear. Both Will and I knew enough to keep quiet.

We traveled until nightfall, then camped beside a rocky bed that once held a sprawling river. Now it was a gully with earthen walls, the rocks worn smooth and flat, forming a natural barrier to the east. Although there was no water, the way across was still treacherous and slow. Nasri said we would wait for morning to continue the journey.

He didn't feed us, but one of his men took pity and gave us a few scraps and two bottles of water. We ate with our hands tied behind our backs, chewing at our food like animals. Because Will's leg hurt worse than before, I held his bottle between my knees and opened the top with my teeth. We were too tired to talk and fell asleep huddled against each for warmth.

In the morning Nasri brought us breakfast, along with two pills for Will's injury. His mood had improved, which made me worry.

Sure enough he announced we were heading to an auction where we would fetch top dollar—not enough to replace the carrier, but more than enough for a new desalinator.

"And with the money Bluewater owes us, we'll have another carrier in no time," he declared.

I felt the prickly tendrils of unease on my neck. There was something unholy about the relationship between the corporate desalinator and the environmental group.

"Why does Bluewater owe you money?"

"That's for me to know and you to find out," he cackled.

"Shouldn't it be the other way around?"

"Should be!" He was hopping again.

"You had their desalinator, but you said *they* owed *you* money."

"Genius! It's a shame we had to take you out of school."

"I thought environmentalists believed desalination was bad for the environment."

A scowl crossed his face but then passed. "Haven't you learned anything by now? What's good for the environment isn't always good for environmentalists, and vice versa." He was in a fine mood, hopping from one foot to the other as if he were standing on hot coals.

Will had been watching our conversation carefully, like a spectator at a gaming match. Now our eyes locked, and I could see he was truly frightened. I was frightened too, but I plunged ahead. Talking was the only way I knew to keep fear at bay.

"So you're hypocrites," I said.

"If there's money in it." Nasri cackled again.

"Did you kill Dr. Tinker for money?"

"Of course. Why else kill a man?"

Then it came to me in a moment of clarity. "Bluewater paid you to kill Dr. Tinker."

"Not enough." Nasri stopped hopping. "Let's just say there was some renegotiating once we had him."

"But why?"

"Ours is not to question why," said Nasri. "We just cash the credit chips."

"And the dam?"

"A diversion. To spirit the good doctor away."

"You killed all these people for a diversion?"

"Oh, and to save Earth, of course."

The pirates, PELA, and now Bluewater all wanted Dr. Tinker. But it wasn't Tinker they had really wanted; it was what they had thought he would lead them to. And now he was dead, which meant only one thing. I felt like I had been kicked in the heart.

"I'd rather kill a man than kidnap him anyway," Nasri continued. "Simpler, and you don't have to deal with grieving relatives. Just dump the body and move along."

I didn't answer, and Nasri seemed disappointed by my silence. But my stomach was knotted, and I couldn't talk even if I had wanted to. After several attempts Nasri stopped trying. "It's a shame to lose you," he said. "You're such a cute girl."

I flinched, but he had already turned for the door. When it closed we were in darkness again.

"Vera?" asked Will.

"Bluewater has Kai."

"You don't know that."

"I do." Anyone who knew the location of the river was a threat to Bluewater and its water monopoly. That was why it had paid PELA to kidnap Dr. Tinker. The desalinating companies were like countries unto themselves—fighting for territory and power. Just as nations profited from surpluses, they profited from shortages and scarcity. But they wouldn't have killed Dr. Tinker if they had thought he was still useful.

I could feel the hover-carrier lifting off the ancient riverbed. Time seemed to have slowed; each second was like the space between drops of water. In between the drops I could feel my friend's absence.

"They're going to kill him, Will."

"No, they won't. Why would they? Think about it logically, Vera. If Bluewater went through the trouble to kidnap him from his home, why kill him?"

I wanted to believe Will was right, but I knew he wasn't. If Dr. Tinker was dead, it meant Bluewater no longer needed him. If they no longer needed him, it meant they knew the location of the river, or had Kai, or both. Soon they would not need Kai either.

I sank to the floor of the carrier. My hands were still tied behind my back, so I curled into an awkward ball, my feet facing one direction, my head and knees in the other. Will sidled up beside me and nudged my shoulder onto his thigh. His ripped trousers still smelled faintly of chemo-wash, the brand our father kept buying even after our mother could no longer do the laundry.

We stayed that way for a long time. The carrier swooped and

dipped, crossing the wrecked and forsaken land. Below us were hectares of parched earth, fissured and broken without a trace of green. A dazzling sun illuminated metallic yellows, grays, and blues: mercury, lead, cadmium. The air was dusty and glittered gold with thousands of particles swirling in the wind. I dozed, or thought I did, my mind jumbled and disjointed like confetti.

When the carriers finally stopped, it was late afternoon. The rear doors were flung open, and the cargo hold was bathed in a sudden chill. A lone horn sounded in the distance. It made me shiver. "Where are we?" I asked Will.

"Welcome to Niagara!" said Nasri from the rear steps. "Enjoy the honeymoon!" His laugh was brittle and thin.

I rose slowly and helped Will off the floor. We stood unsteadily, blinking in the harsh light. Nasri scampered into the cargo hold, followed by two of his men who were dressed as if for combat: boots, kev-jackets, pistols tucked in waistbands. He signaled to them, and one of them grabbed Will, while the other took firm hold of my arm.

"Normally we'd get more for you," Nasri said, squeezing Will's cheek between his forefinger and thumb. "But your sister here is feisty, and there is that nasty wound on your leg."

"You can't sell us!" I said.

"See what I mean?" said Nasri. "Feisty!"

"How much are they paying you?" I asked. "Our father will pay you more."

"I thought your parents were dead. Besides, we've come too far to ransom you back to your family."

Outside, the horn sounded again, and the men tightened their grips.

"Do not ask for whom the bell tolls…" said Nasri, and then there was that cackle again.

"What's going to happen to us?"

"You will become quite excellent shimmiers, capable of disappearing into the narrowest hole. Then you will be sold off to mercenaries to fight in the war."

Will's face was pale and covered in a sheen of perspiration. He gripped my elbow unsteadily. But he stood on his two feet and spoke in a clear, strong voice.

"You won't get away with this," he said.

"But I will," said Nasri.

"Then you should hope we die here. Because if we don't, one day I'll be old enough, and I will hunt you down and kill you."

Nasri smiled, but his brown eye twitched. "Tough words for such a skinny boy. I suppose I *should* kill you now."

"Do it," said Will. "It's your last chance." He stared back at Nasri fiercely.

I couldn't believe Will was talking to Nasri this way, daring him to kill us. Nasri was just crazy enough to do it—we had already seen him shoot Dr. Tinker. But he didn't even remove his pistol from his waistband.

"I hope you live long enough to follow through on your plans," Nasri said. Then he signaled to his men, and they followed him from the hold, dragging us like old luggage.

Nothing prepared me for the scene that greeted us when we stepped from the carrier. If someone had told me we were on the moon, I wouldn't have doubted it. The land was pocked and cratered, with holes as large as entire canyons. Though the sun was shining, it was through a dusty haze, weak and distant. Giant machines, which at first I thought were buildings, perched beside mountains of rocks and sand. A bone-rattling wind blew, and it carried a stench that was indescribable and yet horribly familiar: a metallic smell, like sticking your head into a venti-unit, or being buried alive. It was the smell of sickness, disease, and death.

Most striking, however, were the children: thousands of them scrambling over the piles of dirt or shimmying down into crevices between rocks. Deep in the canyon bottom, they scurried from drill hole to drill hole, emerging into the gloom like colonies of insects.

They were sick. I could see it even from a distance. Though some wore shields, they could not cover watery inflamed eyes, swollen lips, bloody noses, open scabs, and pus-filled wounds. Some were missing fingers, and others were missing entire limbs. Many were bald or balding, and every now and then, one would collapse and lay still.

"What is this place?" I whispered.

"It used to be a great waterfall," said Nasri.

I'd heard about Niagara in school. So much water rushed from the mountains that it poured off the shelf of the land into the giant canyon. The power of the waterfall generated enough electricity to light an entire city, and the people who lived there grew rich and prosperous. Then oil replaced water as the cheaper form of power, and the people fled while the city deteriorated. Now water meant great wealth again, except it had been squandered and wasted, and all that remained was trapped hundreds of meters below ground.

Nasri repeated the story to us. He seemed to take pleasure in his history lesson. It was as if it gave him a sense of superiority to recount the foolishness of people who had thought their resources were endless. In dangerous times, people like Nasri ruled. They cared little for grand ideals, but much more for survival. They watched their backs and wielded quick knives. Their lives were nasty, brutish, and short.

"And the children?" I asked.

"Waiting for Santa Claus," said Nasri.

His men shoved us roughly toward a tin-roofed compound that appeared to be the office or headquarters of whoever ran the drilling operation. Will dragged his bad leg while I tried to slow down so he could keep up. Although we passed several groups of children, none looked at us. There wasn't a single one who appeared healthy. Even those with all their limbs and digits had open wounds on the backs of their hands or arms and scabby spots on their heads where their hair was missing. I tried to get Will's attention, but he was staring at the children, his mouth open in horror.

I was interrupted by the sight of a tall man who appeared from the trailer with two armed guards. He seemed to know Nasri, and the two men exchanged greetings while the guards watched warily. Then he stepped over toward Will, took his lower jaw in his hand, and cast an appraising glance over the length of his body.

"What happened to this one?" he asked.

"Leg wound. He'll be fine. It's healing nicely."

The man grunted and tore open the rest of Will's trouser leg with a knife. His wound looked worse than before, more green than red and moist with fluid. The man poked at it with the tip of his knife, and Will winced visibly but remained silent.

"No worse than anyone else," concluded the man.

Then he approached me, and I could smell his stink before he was within arm's length. There was no way to describe it except to say that he had obviously never wasted any chemicals on cleaning himself. He was rancid, and I couldn't help gagging.

"You'll grow used to it," he said. "They all do." He lifted my head by my hair, then pulled down my eyelids with a thick blackened finger. "Good root tone," he said. "I'll take 'em both."

"They're fifty credits each."

"I'll give you forty for them both."

"Seventy-five."

"Fifty."

"Deal."

The man pulled out a wireless device from his rear pocket and beamed the transaction to Nasri's handheld.

The entire encounter had taken no more than a minute, and suddenly we were locked in the strong grip of two guards. "There's nowhere to run," said the man. "You'll learn that soon too."

As bad as things had been, they were now worse. This was a prison camp disguised as a drilling operation, and I was certain the money that had just changed hands was not merely for free labor. Other horrors awaited us, deadly and unknown.

"Nasri!" I called out.

He stopped and turned around. "What is it?" he asked. His hand was already on the key pad of the hover-carrier.

"I don't believe you are a bad man."

"But I am."

"Don't you have any kids of your own?"

"None that I care about."

He turned and raised a finger to punch the code on the hover-carrier door pad.

A thumping sound like a thousand birds beating their wings at the same time interrupted him, while a sharp and violent wind spat sand across the sky. I looked up, but the wind filled my eyes with tears. A rocket scorched overhead, and the lead hover-carrier exploded in flames. Machine gun fire ripped the air. Nasri screamed as the door shredded in his hands. His men dropped to their knees to return fire, but bullets cut through their kev-jackets as though they were blankets.

Smoke, shrapnel, pandemonium, and death were everywhere. I reached for Will, and we flung ourselves to the ground—with nothing but rubble to save us.

CHAPTER 13

The helicopter hovered fifty meters above the ground, firing short bursts from its mounted guns. The ground exploded in shattered rock. Nasri's men ran for cover behind the wreck of the hover-carrier, but they were easy prey for the guns that picked them off like targets on a screen. Their small arms fire fell harmlessly back from the sky, and they were quickly silenced.

The two surviving carriers sped off into the desert with the copter in pursuit. The carriers were fast, but the helicopter was faster, and it caught the first one about three kilometers downriver. With two rockets it left the carrier a smoldering hulk in the sand. Even from a distance, Will and I could see orange flames lick the ground while black smoke curled into the sky. The other carrier was luckier. It raced in the opposite direction and soon disappeared beyond the range of the copter. The pilot circled overhead with no chance of pursuit. Nose bowed low and blades rotating slowly, the copter made its way back to the site.

The canyon floor was deserted. The massive drilling machines worked unattended like robots on an alien planet, mining for water below the dead lake's surface. The walls of the canyon reverberated with the sound of metal grinding rock. Gray dust floated in the air, coating everything with a ghostly pallor. Even the guards had disappeared, retreating underground like snakes.

The copter landed on the abandoned floor. I peered out from behind the small pile of rocks that had protected us as the door popped open and the pilot emerged. He was followed by another man about fifteen centimeters taller and ten kilos heavier. The pilot was tattooed up his bare arms and open vest, and even his helmet had decals and insignias. The other man, however, was unadorned, except for a single small tattoo of a bird on his neck.

"Ulysses!" I cried. I ran from the hiding place before Will could stop me.

Ulysses turned toward the sound of my voice. When he saw me, he dropped to one knee and raised his arms. I ran right into him, throwing my hands around his thick neck. His chest was warm and full, and I buried my head in the rough fabric of his shirt.

"I thought you were dead," I whispered.

"I thought *you* were dead!" he roared.

I hugged him harder and was surprised at how good it felt. It had been a long time since I had hugged anyone like that, and I held on tightly. Finally I stepped back and looked at him. There was a new wound on his forehead, and when I touched it gently, he flinched.

"That's the worst of it," he said. The story tumbled out of his mouth in a rush: After the dam had burst, he had been knocked unconscious and awoke in the truck, one leg wedged under the seat and his arms tangled in wire. Somehow he hadn't drowned, and the truck had been pushed by the waters to drier ground. He had managed to extricate his arms and leg, then to crawl through the open door and collapse. The helicopter had found him lying on the ground about half a kilometer from the truck, nearly dead of dehydration even though the waters from the dam still flowed nearby.

Most of the pirates' equipment had been destroyed, and at least half his men were dead or missing. The dogs were gone, and he assumed they were dead too. Only two trucks still functioned, and the pirates had salvaged parts for a third. Ulysses left the survivors to repair what they could while he and the pilot took off to search for Will and me. They ambushed some of Nasri's men on the road, and from them they learned we were in the canyon.

"We couldn't leave you in the hands of PELA," he concluded.

I never felt more grateful to have been captured by pirates. But the loss of my new friends weighed heavily again: Ali, Pooch, and Cheetah. Death was everywhere, but never so sudden or so violent. The images of swollen bodies taken by the river haunted me, faces purpled and blackened tongues extended. I would never forget the sight of blood spurting from Dr. Tinker's head, dark red and viscous. I shut my eyes, but the dead were still there: hands twisted, legs akimbo, mouths frozen in horrible screams. But I didn't see Kai, and that gave me the slimmest hope.

Will had stood quietly nearby, listening to Ulysses's story, and now he ventured closer. "What about the driller?" he asked. "The driller and his son?"

"Kai?" asked Ulysses.

I tried to hide my surprise but could not. Ulysses laughed and said, "I'm not a dunce. You gave it away the first day we met you.

Then we heard you talking in the truck. Of course we know Rikkai. I told you we were following him."

"You said you were following a boy and his father."

"The father goes where the boy tells him."

Was Kai alive? I felt my heart quicken.

"He's a diviner," explained Ulysses. "Finds water with his nose. And he's found something big."

"His nose?" repeated Will.

"That's the theory, but there are lots of them. Doesn't matter how he does it. The fact is, he can find water, and his father drills for it."

He can find water. I remembered the way Kai first spilled water on the road, as if he knew there was plenty more where it came from. The gifts he brought to our home. How he found the underground spring at the abandoned mill. *He can find water.*

"Is Kai here then?" asked Will.

Ulysses shook his head. "No. This is an evil place. It's all dried up. In a couple months, the final aquifer will fail. The men will try to hide it by adding chemicals to the water that remains, but after a while even that will become too expensive, and they'll abandon it."

"What will happen to the kids?" I asked.

Ulysses's mouth drew tight. "They'll die. Or the men will shoot them and bury them in the caves. I've seen it happen."

"We have to help them!"

Ulysses did not respond, but children began emerging from the caves and drill holes, drawn by the helicopter, the lack of gunfire, and a constant driving thirst.

"There are too many," said the pilot, speaking for the first time.

"We can try."

Now there were more children, hundreds of them, perhaps even thousands, standing on the edges of the entrances to the caves, staring back. I could feel their eyes, curious and burning, beseeching me. We had to save them.

Ulysses put his hand on my forearm. "The most we can do is free them from here, give them some water, and hope they make it on their own."

"They'll die. You said so."

"We don't have a choice."

I was about to argue, but Ulysses raised his gun. I looked to where he was aiming, and saw the tall man with his two guards approaching. Two other guards were about twenty meters behind them. Ulysses gently pushed me backward toward Will and the pilot.

"Put down the weapon," instructed the man.

Ulysses adjusted his grip and sighted through the laser.

"You're outnumbered," the man continued. "Drop your weapon."

"Outnumbered on the ground. There's a bird in the air will take out all of you before you can get off a single shot."

The tall man considered this. "And where is this bird?"

"She's silent, but you'll hear her if you don't lay down your guns."

The man smiled, but it was clear he was nervous as he looked from Ulysses to the sky and back to Ulysses again. Perhaps Ulysses was bluffing, but pirates were known to surprise their foes, and there was already one helicopter responsible for a dozen dead bodies.

"Better come with us, then," said the man, and he took one step toward Ulysses.

Before I could take my next breath, the man was on the ground clutching his leg. Ulysses dropped and rolled, then came up firing at the two guards by his side. One went down immediately, while the other spun backward, his hands trying to hold in the blood spilling through the belly of his tunic. The other two guards rushed forward, and one managed to get off a shot, but a round from Ulysses plugged him in the chest and dropped him where he stood. The other never got off a shot.

This all happened quicker than the eye could follow. When it was over, my feet had barely moved. A stray bullet had split a rock not more than one meter away, and a dusting of chips and the smell of cordite still hung in the air.

The pilot quickly tended to the two wounded men, while Ulysses confirmed the other four were dead. The man Ulysses had shot in the gut was moaning softly, and the pilot signaled he wasn't going to make it. Ulysses took the man's pulse, then held his head while he whimpered and gurgled blood. When the man died, Ulysses gently closed his eyelids with his fingers. Then he turned to Will and me.

"Everyone all right?"

I nodded, still trying to sort through what I had just seen.

"Where did you learn to shoot like that?" asked Will.

"I've learned a lot of things I wish I hadn't."

Will just kept staring at Ulysses. I know he was thinking about the shootouts at the gaming center, except this one was brutal and real, and the dead did not get up and play again. Ulysses wiped his bloodstained hands on his pants, and then pushed his sweat-matted hair off his forehead with the back of one palm. His hand, I noticed, was shaking.

"There was no bird, was there?" I asked.

"Oh, yes, there was," said Ulysses, touching the tattoo on his neck. "Her name's Miranda."

I understood everything then. I could see every line in the pirate's craggy face. His skin was sunburned and dry. His ears were cracked and bloodied. But his brown eyes were like dark pools in which fantastic creatures swam.

"What happened to her? To Miranda?"

Ulysses shrugged. "What happens to most children. She got sick, and never got better."

"And your wife?"

"The same."

"But you said you were married," said Will, glancing down at Ulysses's ring, smooth and lustrous in the half-light.

"I'll always be married. But it'll be the next world when I see her again."

Our father believed in Heaven, but I thought it was a place that shakers pretended existed—without it there would be too many other questions. Ulysses, however, seemed confident he would see his wife and daughter again. And maybe, I thought, the belief was all that mattered.

The children had drawn closer now. There were several of them who seemed older and more confident than the others, and they approached Ulysses.

"Please, mister," said one. "Do you have any food?" He was nearly as tall as Ulysses but less than half his weight. Clumps of hair grew from his head in no discernible pattern, and his eyes were bloodshot and rheumy. Ulysses asked his name, and the boy said he was called Thomas and the girl next to him was Danielle. I was shocked to hear Danielle was a girl; she looked almost identical to Thomas: same hair, same height, same sickly bodies. They were, in fact, brother and sister, Thomas said.

"Where are your parents?" I asked.

Thomas shrugged. "Dead, we think." He explained their town had been raided by Mounties, because the residents were siphoning water from a pipeline. The adults were shot; the town burned; and the children taken prisoner to the canyon.

"Most of us are dead now," he concluded.

I looked at Ulysses, and I knew he knew what I was thinking.

"There's nothing we can do," he said again.

"Yes there is," I insisted. "Give them the canyon."

"Give it to them?"

I opened my arms and stretched them tip to tip, north to south. "The drilling site. The machinery. The trucks. The weapons. Everything."

"They wouldn't survive for a minute."

"You said they won't survive anyway."

Ulysses rubbed his chin and frowned. "I suppose a mounted gun might help." He glanced at the helicopter.

"There's a weapons room in the main building," Thomas said.

"And a cold storage with food," said Danielle, the first words she had spoken.

"There's water too," I added.

Ulysses sighed, but he knew he had been outmaneuvered. He signaled the pilot to bring him the prisoner. When the tall man was before him, Ulysses grasped him by the edges of his collar. "The keys," he said.

"No keys," the man managed. "Tumblers."

"The combination, then."

The man hesitated, and Ulysses cocked his weapon and pointed it at the man's head. "You smell bad," he said. "I doubt you'll be missed."

The man stuttered, then quickly gave up the code. Ulysses sat him back on the ground and called for Thomas.

"You know how to fire this?" he asked.

Thomas took Ulysses's gun. It looked absurdly large in his thin hands, but he released the safety like a professional. "My father taught me," he explained.

"Good." Ulysses turned to the man kneeling before him. "This boy's in charge now. You'll do as he says. If you don't—as you can see, his father taught him how to shoot you."

Dozens of other children had drawn closer, curious and hungry—vacant eyes calculating the risks, weighing whatever Ulysses had to offer. He coaxed them nearer and singled out several of the biggest, healthiest boys to accompany him to the helicopter. There they withdrew the mounted gun from its bay, and carried it to the front of the main building. Then they went back and forth several times with boxes of ammunition and crates of grenades. Will and I helped until the building was well-fortified and well-armed.

The throng of children pushed in on us, and I worried they might riot. They didn't smell as bad as the foul man, but they didn't smell good either. My grip on Will was loosening, and I felt a mounting panic as the children swelled around me. They pushed and shoved and seemed to come from everywhere.

Then Ulysses's voice split the crowd. "Dinner!" he announced.

A great roar erupted as Ulysses pushed Thomas toward the caves. The boy ran, not like something sickly, but something spectacular, his hair flaming and triumphant, his sister, Danielle, behind him, followed by scores of children of all sizes, the smallest carried by the tallest, the crippled guided by the able-bodied. They spilled into the caves like an ancient river, a stream of humanity drawn by the promise of food, nourishment, life itself.

In a moment Will and I were alone with Ulysses and the pilot. Dust from hundreds of footsteps still hovered in the air. A weak sunlight pushed through. The atmosphere was rank, but a breeze had begun to blow. We had given the children what we could to protect and feed them. The rest was up to them.

Ulysses stepped toward the helicopter. "Ready?" he asked.

"For what?" asked Will.

"To find Kai, of course."

CHAPTER 14

We flew south.

From the sky, the earth looked like a flattened soy cake. The blues, greens, and whites familiar from the school screens were missing, as if they had always been a lie. At fifteen hundred meters I could see dried rivers like the spidery, cracked fingers of a dead man. The only thing of color was a brilliant red sun, burning low in the west.

On the ground I had never thought much about the earth, but from the sky it was all I could see. We could have been on Mercury or the moon, some barren place that creatures had once inhabited but now were long gone. Not a single living thing stirred, and the ever-present grayish dust spiraled in thousands of eddies. I saw something that could have been a road, but it was decomposed and swallowed up on either side. The remains of a truck or a tank were scattered like bones nearby. In the copter it was drier even than on land, and I couldn't lick my lips quick enough to keep them moist.

I knew if we could climb higher, I would see the silver pearls that dotted the planet's surface and were all that remained of the great lakes and rivers. Enormous reservoirs, they held all the fresh water left on the planet. Canals, aqueducts, pipes, and pumping stations funneled every drop into their well-guarded steel and concrete basins. Humans had finally made the world to suit their purposes. Even the weather was under their control, and the sun, moon, and stars were sure to follow.

A chill made my bones ache and muscles shudder.

"There's another blanket in the rear," said Ulysses.

Will reached for it and handed it to me. I let it fall to my lap. "How do you know he's there?" I asked.

"Don't know for certain," said Ulysses. The PELA mercenary who had told the pirates Kai was a prisoner of Bluewater had traded the information for his life. To him, Kai was just a boy and well worth the trade. PELA did the dirty work and asked no questions.

"So what's your plan?" asked Will.

"The plan?" Ulysses chuckled. For the first time, I noticed that his clothes were ragged and torn. His unwashed hair and unshaved beard made him look like the older men in the gaming center. When he grinned, his crazed and cracked smile framed a handful of battered yellow teeth. But his brown eyes glittered like a promise. "Save the kid. Find the water. Get rich."

"Seriously. Don't you have a plan?" I asked.

Ulysses tried to look serious for a minute. "I thought you were the smart one," he said. "Don't *you* have a plan?"

"You can't just fly into the Great Coast, shoot your way into Bluewater, and take Kai and his father," I told him.

"Why not?"

"'Cause you can't. They'll kill you, for one thing."

Ulysses scratched his beard. "Hmm. Need a better plan."

The pilot interrupted with a question about their route, and he and Ulysses reviewed our position against a crinkled and torn map. We were flying low, and now there were the unmistakable signs of habitation: broken roads, scavenged vehicles, the ruins of concrete buildings, smashed and flat as if they had been crushed by a giant foot. But no people, and no other signs of life.

"The cities were the first to go," said Ulysses, noticing that I was staring out the window.

"Why?"

"Most of them have no water. They piped it in from the country. There were riots and war."

"The Great Panic."

"Before that, even. The Panic came later. When the Canadians dammed the rivers and the last great polar cap melted."

"They melted it for water," said Will, who pushed himself forward so that he was practically sitting on my seat.

"It was already melting. The ice caps were retreating, and the sea did the rest."

"Why didn't anyone stop it?"

"They couldn't. It happened too quickly, and it was too warm. Countries took what they could. But when the ice caps melted, all that water was wasted—it spilled into the sea and turned to salt. The aquifers had already dried up. The lakes had been drained or poisoned. All that was left were the rivers, and most of those were already dammed."

"What about the rain?" I asked. "The sky."

Ulysses nodded slowly. "There should be enough rain for everyone. But there isn't. We've dammed the clouds too."

Now I could see something gray off in the distance. At first I thought it was a landing strip, but as we got closer, it spread to the horizon, and flecks of white appeared on its surface. It was water, I realized, as far as the eye could see, to the edge of the earth and beyond. We had seen pictures of the ocean in school, of course, but the photos couldn't capture the vastness of the unbroken plain, or its emptiness. Earth was mostly water, yet nearly all of it was undrinkable. During the Great Panic, the coastal cities suffered most. Looking at the unbroken stretch of grayish-green, it seemed as if all of man's problems could be solved if only we could drink from the ocean. But we couldn't.

Then I saw something else: a blue octagon resting on the sea. It appeared first like an indistinguishable point on a darkened background, but as we got closer, it resolved into eight sides, like a giant blue spider, each with an oversized silver pipe that stretched into the ocean. I could see as well that it wasn't actually on the ocean. It sat above the water on steel stilts that the waves could not touch.

"What is that building?" I asked, though I suspected I knew the answer.

"Bluewater," confirmed Ulysses. "That's where they do their magic."

The global desalination company's magic came with a price. Desalination was more expensive than most countries could afford, and large-scale desalination poisoned the oceans with minerals, chemicals, and sludge. Yet just as humans might turn to cannibalism if they were hungry enough, governments turned to the sea for their water. Soon companies like Bluewater were more wealthy and powerful than any nation, and anyone who could afford the price lived with a steady source of water.

"It's more taking without giving," Ulysses concluded. "Someday they'll pay."

The helicopter dipped left, and my stomach dropped. But what I saw next made me sick with worry. A jet in the near distance, close enough that I could see the Bluewater emblem—a black spigot superimposed over a blue wave. It rocketed low in the sky, then banked toward us.

"Ulysses," I whispered.

But he had already seen the jet, and he barked quick instructions to the pilot. The helicopter swooped back to the right, but there was no way to outrun a jet. The next time, it passed so close that I could actually see the pilot in the cockpit. He wore a black and blue helmet with an oxygen mask over his mouth, and his eyes were covered by something see-through and metallic. He dipped his wings twice, signaling us to land, but the helicopter pilot ignored him.

"Fly inland," Ulysses instructed.

The helicopter turned from the ocean and raced over the land. The jet kept pace, crisscrossing the sky above us and repeatedly dipping its wings. Once we even saw the pilot make a landing motion with one of his hands, but Ulysses and his pilot ignored him.

"They're going to shoot us down," said Will matter-of-factly.

"Not yet," said Ulysses.

Now the helicopter was over a thick field of geno-soy, a crop that was irrigated with water from the desalinating factory. The plants looked withered and brown, but I knew they had been genetically altered to require as little water as possible, which allowed them to survive in harsh conditions. The fields stretched as far as I could see without a retractable roof or any sign of evaporation management. They rippled in the wind from the rotors, bending like waves in a storm. Their beauty was transfixing and held my eye as the horizon disappeared.

The shadow of the jet moved swiftly across the ground. It bore down on us before I saw it in the air. There was a puff of smoke from beneath one of its wings and a missile flew at us with deadly accuracy.

"Ulysses!" I screamed this time.

There was no time even to blink. The missile exploded in a ball of fire just one hundred meters from the nose of the helicopter. It knocked us sideways and threw Will and me to the floor, but the copter remained in the air.

"A warning shot," said Ulysses. Then to the pilot: "Take us down before they straighten their aim."

We scrambled back into our seats, and this time we buckled ourselves in securely. If there was a place to land, I didn't see it. But the pilot hurried to the ground as if he did. Too fast! We were coming in too fast! We couldn't land at this speed!

There was a terrific ripping noise and a spine-shattering crash. The windows blew out, and everything inside flew outside. The safety harnesses cut deeply into our shoulders, and the backs of the seats were like hard rubber mallets against our heads.

The hush that followed was the stillness of death. Ulysses was the first to speak. "Vera? Will? Roland?"

Will's voice was soft but clear. My head hurt, but as far as I could tell, nothing was broken or bleeding. The pilot, however, was silent.

"Roland?" Ulysses repeated.

The pilot's body was not in the helicopter—or what was left of the metal wreckage. I craned my head to see that Will was still strapped into his seat, although the steel trusses on which the seat had been fastened were ripped from the bottom of the helicopter's frame. Ulysses was pinned between the door and the roof and struggling to free himself. But there was no sign of Roland.

Then I saw him, lying in the geno-soy about twenty meters from the left door. His head was snapped back at an unnatural angle, and one arm was twisted beneath him. I knew he was dead before I even noticed the bright red pool that stained the brown plants. Bile rose in my throat, and I forced down a strangled cry.

"What is it?" asked Ulysses.

"He's dead," I sputtered.

"No time for mourning," he said. "Help me out of here."

Will slipped from his safety harness and climbed through the twisted debris to help Ulysses. "He needs a proper burial!" Will exclaimed.

"Can't wait for that."

As if to punctuate his words, the jet roared overhead. White contrails in the sky; a light mist like rain.

"Have to get moving," said Ulysses. "They won't leave us alone for long."

I released my seat beat and felt a stabbing, electric pain through my shoulder. Before I could stand, I fell to the ground.

Will was next to me, and then Ulysses. His brisk and indifferent demeanor suddenly melted. "What is it, little sister?" he asked.

"My shoulder," I managed.

Ulysses gently manipulated my arm. The pain was like a thousand knives in an open wound. "Dislocated," he concluded. "I can fix it, but it will hurt worse first."

"How much worse?"

"Like stretching the muscle until it tears."

"And then it will feel better?"

"Yes."

"Do it."

Ulysses looked at me long and hard, as if he were weighing the pain against his ability to inflict it.

"Give me your hand," he said.

He took my good arm and gripped it tightly. The hard calluses on his palm scratched my skin. His other hand was on my shoulder. His chest was pressed close up against me. I could see every line in his face, the fine hairs on his cheeks above his beard where no beard grew. I could feel the thumping of his heart, the hard steady rhythm that matched mine. He steadied himself with a deep breath and turned away. Then he pulled.

The pain was like nothing I had ever experienced. It was as if every fiber in my arm cried out at once, then was ripped from its anchor. A swirl of violent colors washed over my eyes, and my face burned as if on fire. Then something slipped and fell back into place, and just like that the pain subsided. I was left dizzy and nauseated, covered in a cool, clammy perspiration.

"It's done," said Ulysses.

Then I did vomit, in a wrenching spasm that doubled me over. Nothing but a thin stream of spittle emerged, however, and once it was gone the nausea passed. I wiped my mouth and sat up straight. "I'm okay," I said.

Ulysses tore a strip of cloth from his shirt and tied a makeshift sling from my neck to my wrist. "It's not what the doctor ordered, but it will hold your arm."

Will was staring at me with something like awe. "Did it hurt?"

"Not that much," I lied.

The jet thundered again overhead and dropped two flares into the geno-soy. Plumes of red smoke rose toward the sky.

"They're flagging us," said Ulysses. "Let's get moving." He put an arm around me and helped me stand, then beat a path through the soy with his free hand. The plants were thick and hard to bend, but Ulysses held them down until we could pass. The stalks reached higher than my head. I kept looking up to make sure the sky was above me, but it only made me lose my step, and I still felt trapped and claustrophobic.

After a few minutes, I noticed Ulysses had slowed and was limping.

"You're hurt," I said.

"It's nothing," he said.

But his leg was dark red with blood. It had soaked through his pants and the wound appeared to still be bleeding. I insisted we rest, but Ulysses refused. "In about five minutes, they'll be here with robo-sniffers and guns," he said. "They won't stop until they've caught us. They'll leave the bodies in the fields."

His tone was calm, but there was something in his voice that betrayed him. It took me a moment, but I realized he was frightened, and his fear made me more nervous than anything he could have said.

"These are not ordinary people," he continued. "Pirates steal, and we'll cheat if we need to, but we do it to survive and because our enemies do the same. Even PELA has a code, though they don't always live by it. But Bluewater cares only about money. They don't even care about the water, really. They have no loyalty and don't look out for their own. It's greed, pure and simple. Nothing will stand in their way. Not laws, not governments, and not any pirate with a gun."

"How do we know they haven't killed Kai?" asked Will.

"No. They'll keep him as long as it suits their purposes. The boy is a diviner. That's worth *a lot* of money. He can tell them where water is, and they can keep him from telling others. They won't kill him as long as there's use for that."

"He needs medicine," I said.

"They'll give him that too."

The jet had disappeared now, but there came another sound in the distance, harsh and braying.

"Sniffers," said Ulysses. "Move!"

The three of us were battered, two of us bleeding, but we ran as quickly as we could. Will winced with every step, his leg healing but not healed. Ulysses showed no pain, but his pale face betrayed his injury. My shoulder had begun to throb, and every plant that brushed me was like a whipping.

We were deep in the soy fields. I had never seen so much vegetation. I could practically feel the plants pulsating, exhaling moisture like breathing. Without any protection from the sun or the sky, they flaunted the great wealth of their growers. Even with their genetic alterations, they still wasted enough water to quench the thirst of a large town. But their growers didn't seem to care. They had resources to burn, and the food not only tasted better, it was a potent reminder of their enormous power.

"Run, Vera!" Will urged me forward.

The braying grew louder. We followed Ulysses, who beat at the plants with his powerful arms. The pain in my shoulder was nothing compared to the burning in my lungs, the aching in my sides, and a terrible, drill-like pulsing in my skull.

And then suddenly, without warning, Ulysses collapsed.

For a moment time stood still. It was not possible that the great pirate king could fall. Even when I thought Ulysses had drowned, I never saw his body, and I had refused to accept he might actually be gone. But now there he was, splayed out before us, his pants leg soaked and his face white.

I grabbed his hand. "Ulysses," I begged. "Ulysses."

He looked up at me, and his eyes fluttered slightly.

"You remind me of her," he said.

"Who?" I asked, although I knew.

"She was skinny, like you. She used to call me Poppy."

"Hold on," I said. "Please. We'll get you help. I promise."

And then the sniffers were upon us.

CHAPTER 15

The prison cell was no larger than the back of a flatbed truck. I leaned up against one wall, a dull banging in my head like the headache that comes after a beating. It started low, at the base of the skull, and then worked its way up to the temples and the forehead until it threatened to explode.

"Open the door," commanded a voice from beyond the walls.

The banging stopped, and the great steel door swung open. A nearly hairless man walked into the prison cell. He was as tall as Ulysses but with no eyebrows, eyelashes, or beard. His eyes were a pale gray-blue, and he might have been albino, except his skin was a sun-ripened brown. Behind him, hopping on one foot, his face scarred and ravaged, was Nasri. He seemed as excited to see us as we were surprised to see him.

"That's them," said Nasri. "The pirate and his spawn."

The hairless man practically filled the room. Although he was the most unusual man I had ever seen, the most curious thing about him was his shiny fingernails. It looked as if he painted them with polish. There was no trace of dirt, and there were no scabs or other visible injuries on any of his fingers. In fact, as I observed him, I noticed how clean his entire body appeared, and as he approached,

I smelled a scent that reminded me of flowers—the real ones grown in hydro-vaults, not the fake chemo ones planted about the town.

With one foot the hairless man pushed at Ulysses's prostrate body. Ulysses moaned slightly but did not move.

"This one is injured," he said in a voice liquid and smooth. "Get the medic."

"But Torq," protested Nasri, "he's a pirate."

"And now he's our prisoner. We will not let him die quietly."

Nasri hopped from foot to foot but did not protest. Torq obviously frightened him as much as he frightened me. Nasri's mouth worked silently, as if he were chewing over something. He glared at Will, and his hand went involuntarily to the scar on his face. Then he backed from the cell, never letting us out of his sight until the door closed behind him.

In his absence the room seemed to grow smaller. Torq moved closer.

"Why are you here?" Torq directed his question to Will.

"You brought us here," said Will.

"Where did you get the rotorcraft?"

"Where did you get the jet?"

Torq slammed the wall behind Will's head with such force that I was certain he would break something. He picked Will up by the hair and held him ten centimeters off the ground.

"I. Ask. The. Questions." He spat out each word, then dropped Will back to the ground. "You answer!"

Will stammered out a partial version of the truth: We had been rescued by Ulysses from a drill site and were flying back to a pirate camp.

"Pirates don't rescue children," said Torq, raising one hand as if he might yank Will's hair again.

"We're his children!" I blurted.

Torq looked at me for the first time. I held his gaze. His eyes were like pools of dirty gray water—flat and dangerous.

"That may be useful," said Torq.

Nasri arrived with the medic. He was a small man, skittery and nervous. There was dirt or dried blood on the front of his white tunic. He examined Ulysses quickly and gave him two injections. Ulysses did not stir. The medic cut away his bloody trouser leg with a scalpel. I averted my eyes. The sight of all that blood made me feel faint again. I heard the medic murmuring about *sepsis* and *shock*, but I put my head in my hands and blocked the sound.

There was some more cutting, and then some stitching. Another shot. Bloodied medi-pads discarded on the floor. A second medic wheeled a gurney into the room. Both men heaved Ulysses onto the bed.

"Where are you taking him?" I asked.

"Don't you worry," said Torq. "He'll be better in no time. Then we'll stick pins in him until he bleeds again." Torq and Nasri laughed, and the medics wheeled Ulysses out of the cell. Nasri gave us a last violent look, then the steel door clanged shut behind both men, and Will and I were alone in the tiny cell.

"They're going to torture him!" I cried.

"No, they won't," said Will. "Not right away. Didn't you hear them? They need him awake."

"So they can torture him!"

"That gives us time," said Will. "Wherever they've taken him, I'll bet that's where they've got Kai. If we can find one, we can save the other."

"But we're trapped. It's hopeless."

"You told me not to say that!" Will snapped.

"But it is, Will. It is."

He shook his head. The color had returned to his face, and he looked like the Will who once outraced a boy, three years older, on a dare. The medicine Nasri had given him back at the drilling site must have been powerful stuff, because he stood without much effort or visible pain. "You said Kai was our friend and we had to help him. Well, Ulysses is our friend too, and that means we've got twice the people to help, and we've got to work twice as hard."

"But what can we do?"

Will looked around the cell. Except for a small air vent in the ceiling, and window grates in the steel door, the walls appeared solid and impenetrable. There was no handle on the door and no way to open it from the inside. His eyes darted back to the air vent.

"I know what you're thinking," I said. "But even if we knew where that went, we can't possibly reach it."

"Easy," said Will. "Just like condenser duty." He approached the wall, and felt its surface for imperfections. Although it appeared smooth, the wall had hundreds of cracks and fissures—the result of trying to build anything without water. The imperfections were small, but not so tiny that Will's fingers could not grasp them, or his toes without shoes could not find footing.

"Give me a hand," he said.

I made a step by interlocking my fingers and gave Will a tentative boost up the wall. A sharp pain cut into my shoulder, and I staggered backward, but Will had already dug his toes into an open space. He reached out with one hand and felt for the next toehold, then pulled himself up another ten centimeters. In this way he made steady progress. When he approached the corner where the wall met the ceiling, he extended his arm and just barely grasped the vent.

I scurried beneath him. I didn't know if I could hold Will, but I would be there if he fell. I waited while he rested and pursed my lips in silent prayer. I didn't pray about any of the things they taught in school; instead I promised our father that we would return home, no matter what. Will gave one hard yank, and the vent clattered to the floor. Then he pulled himself up and inside. In a moment his face reappeared in the open hole in the ceiling. "There's a passage," he said. "Climb to me." He extended his arm through the hole.

There was no way I could shimmy up the wall as Will had. For one thing, I lacked his strength and agility. For another, my shoulder throbbed badly now, and I knew the effort would rip my arm from its socket. Nevertheless I tried to slip my fingers in the cracks and crawl up the vertical surface. But I had no strength, and the pain was brutal and unrelenting.

"I can't, Will," I cried.

Will undid his shirt and knotted it, then extended it through the hole like a rope. His head was stretched through the vent while his arm dangled the shirt. I leaped and grabbed the end of it with my good arm. But when I tried to pull myself up the wall, I couldn't hold to the crevices. I fell backward and let go, and Will nearly toppled from the ceiling trying to hold on.

I lay on my back on the floor. I did not cry. I was exhausted; we both were. We had traveled nearly two thousand kilometers, crossed several republics and the Empire of Canada, reached the Great Coast, seen hundreds dead, killed several ourselves, starved, thirsted, fought, and were dirtied and bloodied. But we were not dead yet. And neither was Ulysses or Kai.

"You go," I said. "Find the way out, and come back and get me."

It was the only option, and Will knew it. He nodded. "I'll come back. I promise."

Then he was gone.

I sat for a long time on the floor. I listened to the fading echoes of Will's feet overhead and the indistinct rattling of activity occurring somewhere outside the prison walls. If I was very still, I could feel the floor swaying slightly, as if it were moving in a breeze. I thought about all that had happened, each event leading inexorably to the next: if I hadn't seen Kai; if we hadn't become friends; if I hadn't gone to his home; if he hadn't come to mine; if he hadn't told us about the river, or showed me the secret spring; if we'd never kissed. But I also knew many things had been set into motion years before I was born: if there hadn't been the Great Panic; if there hadn't been war; if there had been enough water…Where did it all begin? Our father remembered rivers, but now the rivers were gone. Our mother remembered boat trips and warm baths, but now she was ill. Even Will could remember school before they closed the doors at recess and forbade students from going outside. What did I remember?

Our mother at the kitchen table, laughing at something our father had said. Both our parents, hand in hand, watching the news on the wireless. Climbing into our parents' bed with Will in the morning—the warm blankets and the clean smell of newly sanitized sheets. Will and I running for the bus, screaming madly as we raced to be first. All those memories—once vibrant, now faded. Earth itself changed.

Somewhere in my recollections, I nodded off, and then the memories mixed with dreams and became tangled in half-truths and impossibilities. My mother was lifting me in the air as the clouds spiraled and the sun broke through in curtains of yellow light. *Again,* I cried. *Again!* We twirled and spun beneath the luminous rays. Her head tilted back, my mouth tilted open, spinning, breathing, whirling, alive.

There was a thump and then a bang, and suddenly the outer door swung open.

"Will!"

He turned the handle on the door. "It's not even locked," he muttered with what sounded like disgust. With no knob to open the door from the inside, there was no need to lock it from the outside. But now that it was ajar, I wasted no time joining him.

The hallway was dingy and grimy. No sign of life. The walls were covered in chipped white paint and orange rust. We passed open doors and empty cells. If the prison had held other captives, they were long gone. We moved stealthily toward a pair of double doors at the end of the short hallway. Will put a finger to his lips, although that was unnecessary. My feet glided over the floor without weight or friction. It felt as if my body had escaped gravity, floating just a few centimeters above the surface. Despite the pain in my shoulder and our desperate situation, we had escaped.

Now we were on a steel island, policed by a private army.

We moved like ghosts. Nearby there was water: moisture in the air, on the crease of my neck, in the folds of my elbows and knees. The crinkly, crunchy dryness that was usually my skin felt elastic here, plumped with a thousand invisible molecules. I plucked at the back of my hand, just to make certain, and it sprang back into place without a wrinkle.

When we reached the double doors, they were unlocked. We pushed through into a hallway as clean and white as a medical ward. Even the air had a different smell: freshly filtered and oxidized. Electronic sensors dotted the walls, and there were tiny cameras positioned in the corners. I pointed to one, and Will nodded—he had already seen them. If there were cameras, there were screens somewhere with people watching. But no alarms rang, and no one rushed from the shadows to stop us.

Will hugged the wall, and I followed. The creaking sound was more evident here, and the floors were definitely swaying—it wasn't just my imagination. There was another sound too, like a wireless broadcast. Voices rising and falling, but without the soothing music found in the water conservation programs in the mornings. We moved toward the sound along the wall as it curved, then widened into a common area. The voices became more pronounced: stern, scolding, lecturing, like teachers at school—except no one seemed in charge. They spoke over each other, interrupting and arguing, and no voice took the lead for more than a few moments. I had the feeling it would not end well for the losing side. Will held up one hand, and I stopped, trying not to breathe. My heart thumped as loud as a drum in my chest. From the other side of the hallway, two men emerged into the common area. They wore a dark blue—nearly black—uniform, and their muscles rippled through their shirts. Both had communicators in their ears, security shields dangling from their necks, and heavy firearms on their belts. I squeezed against the wall, trying to press myself into two dimensions. The men were nearly upon us, and I was certain we would be caught and returned to our cells—or worse.

Then there was an electronic squawk, and one of the guards began talking into the air. He signaled to the other guard, and they reversed direction, walking in a heavy-booted fashion back the way they had come. In a moment all was clear.

I relaxed and slid down the wall. Will made certain the guards had withdrawn, and then we eased forward carefully until we reached the common area. There were several couches gathered around a blue glass table and two wireless screens on the wall broadcasting a news feed. The doors were now directly in front of us, and a second set of doors to our right—that's where the voices were. I stayed close to Will, my hand on his elbow. He pushed gently at the release latch, but the doors were locked. There was a small window above eye level, about as high as Will could reach on his tiptoes. He leaned against me for support and stretched.

His slow intake of breath was like the sound as all the air exits a balloon.

"What is it?" I whispered.

But he just shook his head and slowly sank back down on his heels. "You look," he said. He laced his fingers together, and I hesitated, then tentatively placed one foot in his hands. I braced myself with my good arm against the wall, and pushed myself as high as I could climb. Will lifted me until my eyes just cleared the window, and I could make out the mahogany-paneled room with its vases of real fresh flowers and two small trees.

I was not good with politics or government. I wasn't interested in deal-making or brinksmanship, and I couldn't distinguish an undersecretary from an overseer. But there was no mistaking the perfectly coiffed hair of the Canadian prime minister or the sun-baked face of the president of Minnesota. There were also several WABs I recognized from the wireless, and the chief administrator of Arch. His beard was neatly trimmed, and the skin on his face was unnaturally tight, as if it had been screwed onto his skull. At the front of the table was Torq, his smooth head like an egg, hands steepled beneath his hairless chin.

What were they doing here, together in the same room? Sworn enemies, gathered around the table, not fighting but debating, arguing like old friends?

"Hey, you!" a guard's voice bellowed. "Halt!"

CHAPTER 16

We dashed back down the hallway, veering away from the prison wing and heading for a single blue door at the far end that promised Emergency Exit. The guard's communicator squawked loudly, and his boots thumped as he ran after us. Will was limping, and my shoulder ached, and there was no way we could outrun a muscular man even if we weren't both injured.

Will flung the door open. Steel stairs stretched up and down, with no platform in sight. Whichever way we went was a gamble, playing cards we hadn't been dealt. Will went down. I followed. The door clanged shut behind us. We took two steps at a time, our feet skidding on metal. I kept one hand on the railing and the other reaching for Will. My balance precarious, my grip slipping, I fought hard to stay upright.

Despite the sign and the emergency, there appeared to be no exit. The stairs corkscrewed down as far as I could see. Overhead, men shouted, and we heard the heavy clanking of their heels on the stairs. I focused on Will's back, locked on the one thing I could trust. The world compressed into a single point of his spine.

"Here, Vera, quick!" Will commanded.

He stopped so suddenly that we nearly collided. He was

kneeling before an open hatch. It was about thirty centimeters in diameter—no bigger than a mine shaft and just wide enough for a skinny teen.

"What is it?" I asked.

"Water gutter," said Will.

"We don't know where it goes!"

"It goes down!" said Will. That was enough for him. "Come on!"

The men were getting closer. Their squawkings were unmistakable. It was capture or the unknown. I dove. Will followed. Down we plunged. It felt like a nightmare—one of those dreams where you are falling and yet never seem to reach the ground. Arms and legs beyond your control. Eyes unable to focus. I tumbled and banged against the slippery sides, yet nothing slowed my fall.

Then I was suddenly plunged into something cold and liquid, brackish and wet. Water! We were in the ocean! But I had no time to be amazed. I was still falling, and now there was water over my head. I knew I shouldn't breathe, but the urge to take a breath was powerful. I had no idea how to swim, although I knew that's what people used to do. Once there were even giant pools of fresh water for no purpose other than swimming—not even drinking—and athletes played games to see who could swim fastest.

But now I was drowning. Strange: at the time I didn't even know the word. My lungs ached, and my brain felt as if it were burning. I flailed wildly in the water, kicking hard. Seawater went up my nose and stung my eyes. My mouth filled.

I might have died. I should have died. But my flailing propelled me back to the surface, where my head broke through at the last possible moment before I lost consciousness. I gulped in great breaths, bobbing on the surface. The water's abnormal salt content kept me afloat, even though I had no idea how to swim or tread water. I was also sheltered by giant steel piers. From below the enormous structure looked like a hovering spacecraft in bad need of a paint job. The gutter through which we had plunged was just one of an intricate series of pipes, conduits, cylinders, and ducts that sucked in seawater, processed and transformed it, then dispatched it to giant holding tanks while dumping the poisonous residue back into the ocean.

There was a splash, and Will emerged about ten meters away. Like me he had been forced to the surface by enough salt and pollutants to float a small car. It left a taste like licking a metal fence: saline mixed with tin, iron, and rust. He spat and thrashed but managed to stay afloat. I called out to him, and he clawed his way over to me. His swimming wasn't elegant, but it moved him through the water. When he reached me, we embraced: wet hair, wet faces, salty tears in the salty water.

But we weren't out of danger—not yet. Although we were only several hundred meters offshore, we had to fight the currents and several enormous intake drains that sucked water back into Bluewater. We kicked, paddled, and kept our heads above water while the sea eddied around us, churning and swirling and carrying us to land. Finally we collapsed in the black, sulfurous sand, coughing and tearing, our noses running and eyes burning. But alive.

"I don't like swimming," I said after I finally caught my breath.

Will hiccupped a small laugh. "It's not like we're going to be doing it a lot."

"I never want to do it again."

Will didn't disagree. Instead he asked, "Why do you think they're here?"

I knew he was talking about the politicians. I propped myself up on my elbows. "A peace conference?"

Will shook his head slowly. The republics had been at war for so long, it was difficult to imagine peace. And why gather here, at the headquarters of the giant desalinator? PELA, Bluewater, the Canadians, the Minnesotans, and our own chief administrator gathered in the same place where Kai and Ulysses were held prisoner…

"It's Kai," I said.

Will nodded.

"We have to go back."

"I know."

We were both standing now, staring at the spider fortress. We were soaking wet, and our clothes stank. The seawater was contaminated, unfit for any kind of life except the hardiest and the lowest. Neither of us had the energy to venture back the way we had come. Even if we could, then what?

Behind us the black sand gave way to scruffy sparse vegetation, prickly and dry. A broken road that looked as if it hadn't been used in decades cut through to the beach. Beyond, there were a few small ruined buildings, broken signs, abandoned vehicles, and rusted machinery. In the far distance, we spotted wavering gray towers, like a field of concrete grown wild.

"Where do you think we are?" I asked.

"Somewhere on the Great Coast, near what used to be New York City."

"How can you tell?"

Will pointed to the gray shapes in the distance. "Skyscrapers," he said.

I had read about the giant buildings, so tall they scraped the clouds. From the ground they appeared delicate and beautiful, their thin forms spiking heavenward like trees seeking light. I was too far away to see the broken windows or collapsed skeletons, the buildings that lay in piles of rubble on the street. In the Panic the skyscrapers were deathtraps; smoke and fires trapped millions inside. But from the horizon, all was picturesque, peaceful, serene.

"There must be someone in the city who can help us," I said.

"They haven't had water for years. Even if there's anyone alive, there are gangs and criminals and psychos. We would never get out."

He was right. After the Panic, it was said, those who survived in the cities resorted to cannibalism when water wasn't available. I didn't necessarily believe all the stories, but if only a quarter of what we'd heard was true, the cities were still deathtraps. Yet we had no other choice.

"If there are people, there have to be boats," I said, remembering my geography. "Manhattan is an island, and they blew the bridges. We can't get them out of Bluewater without a boat. Ulysses can't swim, and Kai and his father might be injured too."

Will pondered the options. He knew I was right. We couldn't fly a jet or a helicopter, and without something to get from the sea to the shore, we wouldn't travel far.

"How do we find a boat?" he asked. "We can't buy one. If we steal one, we'll never get back here alive."

"We bribe them."

"With what?"

"Water," I said.

We didn't actually have water, of course, but we had the *promise* of water. No thief would kill us if he thought we could lead him to water. But Will wanted to know what we would do when we arrived at Bluewater. Besides, who would be crazy enough to join us? Anyway, it was probably at least a ten-kilometer walk to the city, with barely enough light to make it there before nightfall.

I said we could do it in an hour if we hurried, and the return would be faster with a boat.

We argued until a sound like a broken condenser interrupted us. We looked out, and there was a misshapen egg floating on its side in the water. It appeared squashed at the narrow front end and bulbous and lumpy at the rear. But it moved quickly—faster than seemed possible given its ungainly size. In fact, it wasn't actually in the water at all but hovering above it, creating a wake that traveled in two parallel trenches as the egg—whatever it was—zipped along the surface.

"Skimmer," said Will.

I had never heard of such a thing. Will explained they were fast-moving boats that sucked fresh water from the surface of the ocean using a process similar to desalination. Their great speed filtered the salt water through a membrane that yielded fresh, drinkable water.

"They're not pirates, exactly," said Will. "But they're not legal either."

I waved my one good arm at the skimmer and started shouting. Will grabbed my hand. "What are you doing?"

"They can help us, Will!"

"They'll want water. They'll want Kai."

"So? Isn't that the point?"

Will closed one eye and squinted into the distance with the other. Of course it was dangerous to volunteer Kai—what if he couldn't help, or didn't want to?—but without a boat, we might as well lie down and die on this spit of dirty beach. We were on hostile ground without food, water, or shelter, and night was approaching. Will reluctantly released my hand, and I began waving and shouting again.

The skimmer was doing more than simply sucking the warmest layer of ocean water into its cargo hold. It was circling like a thirsty insect around the pylons that supported Bluewater's headquarters. In fact, as I waved, jumped, and shouted, I realized that the skimmer was trying to suck up the water that spilled back into the ocean as waste from the pipelines. This explained why no other boats tried to stop it and no jets tried to sink it. It was a parasite, living in symbiosis with its host, drinking up its poisons and selling them to others. Cadmium, mercury, thallium, lead—these metals would slowly kill anyone who drank them. But the skimmer ignored us. I waved until my other shoulder ached, then I sank to the sand next to Will.

"It's no use," I said.

Will nodded. His jaw clenched tightly. I could tell that he was in pain. He had been quiet about his leg, but I had seen his grimaces and drawn complexion. The medicine was wearing off. I knew he would not be able to make it all the way to the city.

"Will," I began.

"I'm fine," he said.

"We can rest here for the night."

"We're not resting anywhere. Look at us: We're wet, and we stink. We have no food or water. We won't last a minute out here. You're right: we have to go to the city."

Before we could move two steps, however, a high-pitched whining tore the sky. Two men in dark blue wet suits, each atop a machine that looked like a boxy motorcycle, cut through the top of the waves. Their engines screamed and sprayed foam. They had emerged from Bluewater and were heading toward the beach.

Will saw them too. "They're coming for us," he said without emotion and stood up next to me.

"Shouldn't we run?"

"I'm tired of running."

I took my brother's hand.

The two of us faced the ocean, oddly still as the guards on their moto-skis buzzed toward us. After all the cycling, running, driving, flying, and swimming, it felt good to stand still. Not surrender, because that meant giving up. But defiance and resolve.

The moto-skis drew closer. The noise was as loud as the jet that had pursued us over the soy fields. Each man wore a pair of yellow-tinted goggles and a black breathing mask. The skin around their masks was grayish-green. The ocean was black and brown. The sky was a pale sickly orange.

The machines were fifty meters from the edge of the beach when each man suddenly reared up as if performing a flip, then somersaulted off the back of his ski. The machines continued toward the beach without drivers, fast and furious, roaring up on the sand, grinding and careening and finally crashing into each other. It was all we could do to avoid being struck by rocks and debris before one of the moto-skis burst into flames and the other followed.

The entire incident took less than a few seconds, and neither of us noticed that the top of the skimmer was now open, and a woman stood in the hatchway, a harpoon in her hand.

CHAPTER 17

She said her name was Sula. She stood over us with a tempered steel harpoon, no larger than a sword, but finely honed and deadly sharp. It glinted blue in the afternoon sun. Her arms were exposed in her wet suit, and the muscles twined up her forearms like ropes. Beneath her black cap, her hair was salt-bleached blond, and her eyes were a deep violet-blue. The water still dripped from her suit, and there was blood on her hands.

"You're a long way from the city." Her voice cracked like someone who was not used to speaking.

"We're not from the city," I said.

"No. I can see that." Her gaze was flat and direct and did not linger.

"Did you kill those men?" asked Will.

Sula nodded.

"What will happen to you?"

She shrugged and wiped one hand on her wet suit. "They'll come after me, I expect. They won't find me, and then they'll forget. They usually do."

"Have you killed a lot of men?"

"When I've had to. Women too." She began walking toward the burning moto-skis, and we followed. She picked up some of the scattered debris, examined it, then tossed most of it into the fire. "Bluewater rubbish," she said. "Plasteel and tin."

"Shouldn't we be running?" I asked.

Sula gave me the flat gaze again, efficient and expressionless. "You've got a broken collarbone, and he's got a leg wound. You'll not be running far, I expect."

"Can you take us? In the skimmer?"

"What's in it for me?"

"Water. We know where to find it."

"Not hard to find," she jerked her head toward Bluewater. "They're sucking it out of the sea."

"No. We know someone who knows how to find fresh water. A diviner, they call him."

Sula exhaled sharply through her nose. "I've heard of such a thing. But I don't believe it."

"I've seen him do it," I insisted. "He knows where it flows. They've got him locked up in Bluewater with his father and a pirate king."

"A pirate king!" Sula's lips curled into a slight smile.

"It's true!"

"Stomping your feet won't change my mind."

I was tired, beyond exhausted. The pain in my shoulder was vibrant and aflame. My skin was chafed, chapped, and raw. But I wasn't going to let this harpoon woman scare me, or worse, ignore me. Who did she think she was?

"We'll go back by ourselves, then," I said. I stripped to my underwear and threw my shirt to the sand. Will stared at me, wide-eyed.

"Come on, Will," I said. "We're swimming. And my collarbone's not broken," I added.

Sula's fingers on my forearm were like the keys of an old-fashioned piano, solid and delicate at once. "You shouldn't be swimming in these waters. Not without a wet suit, goggles, and a breathing apparatus."

"I don't care! We have to rescue Kai. And Ulysses." I stood before Sula, hands clenched, breathing hard. Will came up beside me. I really was prepared to swim back to Bluewater, and no one could stop me. I had abandoned reason for pure emotion. It coursed through my blood like holo-sugar, a chemically induced energy infusion. I felt like I could have jumped back into the ocean, chemicals be damned.

"I'll take you in the skimmer," said Sula.

"You will?" Despite my outburst, I was surprised to have convinced this woman of anything.

Sula scooped up my clothes and handed them to me. "I don't like Bluewater, in case it isn't obvious. When I saw those men on their skis—what kind of men kill children? And who knows? If there's fresh water to be had…" She let her voice trail off.

Will grinned at me. I pulled my shirt back on and zipped my trousers. They were wet and uncomfortable, but I barely noticed. We had our boat and hadn't been killed. At least not yet.

But first we had to fit in the skimmer. The boat was barely meant to hold one person. It was rigged to carry as much water as possible and, despite its ungainly shape, designed to be light and quick when empty.

Sula slid into the pilot's seat by ducking under the steering paddles. Once secured, her head could turn only twenty degrees in either direction. A viewscreen clamped to her face gave her a three-dimensional, three-hundred-and-sixty-degree panorama of the outside. Will had to crawl under her legs and wedge himself into the space between the edge of the seat and the back of her knees. In that position Sula could barely reach the control pedals, which limited her ability to stop. Meanwhile I stretched out on Sula's lap with my feet resting against the steering paddles. One accidental push and I could send the boat spiraling in the wrong direction.

What seemed merely uncomfortable and dangerous, however, became nauseating once the skimmer got moving. Each bounce on the waves knocked Will's head against the hard seat. Each dip and crest made my arches ache as I tried desperately not to push the steering paddles. It was so loud in the skimmer that even if we wanted to complain, Sula could not hear us. The venti-unit pumped only enough fresh air for one, and it soon grew stale and rank as odor of our filthy clothes mixed with the smell of fear and sweat.

"Hold tight," said Sula, as if there were something to hold to. The skimmer lurched on the crest of a wave, then tumbled sidelong into a pylon. The collision knocked my head into Sula's chin. I didn't know who had it worse, but my skull felt like someone had driven a stake into it.

"You've got a hard head," she said.

"Not as hard as your chin."

Sula rubbed her injured jaw with one hand as she navigated the skimmer away from the pylon. Then she cut the engines, and the boat bobbed on the waves. When we were directly below a large water-release hatch, she fired a grappling hook that snagged the hatch's metal wheel. The boat steadied in the water, held tautly by the rope. Satisfied that we weren't floating off anywhere, Sula unlatched the outer door of the skimmer, and the three of us climbed onto the deck.

"How do you drive this thing?" asked Will as he examined the bulbous stern and flattened bow.

"I can drive anything," said Sula. "I was raised on a military base. My father flew jets. He taught me to fly when I was still a teenager. After that everything else was easy."

"You can fly a jet?" asked Will with a low whistle of appreciation.

"Anything with an engine," said Sula.

"Is he still in the army, your father?"

"He's dead. Help me with this."

Before Will could ask another question, she flipped him a second coil of rope that he caught with both hands. She knotted the other end and tossed it through an open arm of the hook. Then she grabbed the dangling end and pulled it down, securing another line to the hatch. "Can you climb?" she asked me, holding out the second rope.

I shook my head. I remembered trying to escape the prison cell and Will rescuing me.

"I'll have to carry you, then." She handed the loose rope to Will. "Hold this, and I'll pull you up. When you get to the top, you'll have to open the hatch. Do you think you can do that?"

Will nodded.

"There's no water in it now, so you don't have to worry about that. Turn the hatch hard to the left, and it will pop open. You'll see climbing rungs as soon as you get inside."

Will took the loose rope in one hand and grasped the taut one in his other hand. "Ready," he said.

"Why are you doing this?" I asked.

Sula's eyes were so deep blue that they could have been black. It was impossible to discern where the pupil ended and the iris began. But her eyelashes were a pale and fine gold, lighter than her hair, nearly invisible. When she lifted me into her arms, her eyelids fluttered slightly but never closed. The faintest lines spidered from the corners into the broad plane of her face. I held her, and felt the breath as it went through her lungs.

"It isn't natural, what they're doing here," she finally said.

"Are you a natural-earther?" I asked.

"Never heard of them," she said. "I don't believe in slogans."

Bluewater had factories on the entire coast, she went on. Across the world there were other companies like Bluewater, poisoning the sea so people could turn on the tap without worrying about the consequences. To gain access to water, the lower republics were fighting a war against Canada and the Arctic Archipelago. Across the globe there were other wars between Japan and China, between Australia and New Zealand, between Argentina and the Kingdom of Brazil. Earth existed in perfect balance, but humanity did not.

Sula's words exhausted me, and I suddenly wanted nothing more than to take a nap right there. I slumped in her arms, my body heavy and weary, muscles sapped, without the strength to go on.

"Vera!" Sula pinched my cheeks. Everything was blurred and wavering. I felt myself slipping into darkness, into a deep endless hole. If only I could sleep. But a sharp smell brought me back to consciousness.

Will's face, then Sula's, came into a too-bright focus.

"Smelling salts," Sula explained. "Old-fashioned, but effective. I keep them for when the skimmer gets really bad."

Will knelt beside me. I wished I could have taken a holo of him at that moment and played it for him the next time he kicked me out of his room. He never would believe he was the same brother who had once tried to knock me out with a pillow.

Sula held a bottle to my lips. "She's dehydrated. The salt, the sun, and all that time locked up."

The water was brackish and warm, but nothing had tasted better. I swallowed the whole bottle before I realized how thirsty I was. She handed me a second canteen and cautioned me to drink it more slowly. There was seaweed extract in the water, which gave it the brackish taste, but also replenished lost sugars and electrolytes. "Nothing artificial, but your body's not used to it," she said.

Sure enough I felt faintly nauseated. I put my head between my legs until the feeling passed. Then I stood—a little woozily—with Will and Sula supporting me.

"I can walk," I said, annoyed by all the sudden attention.

Sula smiled and let me go. Will held on a moment longer until I shrugged his arm free. Sula tested the ropes. They held firm. She coiled one end of the first rope into a loose knot around Will's wrist. As she pulled it taut, Will scampered up the second rope to the hatch. I held my breath as he swayed in the wind. Then he reached the top and turned the wheel on the hatch once clockwise, just as Sula had instructed. A quick splash of water doused him, but Sula was right that the drain was mostly empty. He waved down to us and shouted that he was going inside.

With one arm circled around me, Sula gripped the rope. "Ready?" she asked. I nodded. With Sula holding me, I could feel how strong she was. The muscles in her back were nearly as hard as bones. There was no softness anywhere on her body except for her fine, long hair, which had burst free from her cap. It brushed my cheek as we shimmied up the rope.

When we reached the hatch, we followed Will inside. The metal steps embedded in the side of the drain led to the surface, and though there was barely enough room for Sula to squeeze through, Will and I had no problem climbing to the top. We emerged on the steel lower deck—the same deck from which Will and I had just escaped. We stopped to catch our breath and survey the surroundings.

Although it was now closer to winter than summer and we were on the water, the air was warm and still. Two centuries ago the beach would have been chilled and frozen and the water as cold as ice. Now snow was rarer than rain, and frozen seawater was rarer still.

"The holding cells are on sub-three," said Sula.

"They kept us on the main level," I said.

"Those are temporary quarters. The secured level is at sub-three. If they need to extract information, that's where they get it."

"You mean torture?" asked Will.

Sula nodded. Her hand went involuntarily to the harpoons she carried in a rubber satchel that crossed her back. A knife and three canteens hung on a belt around her waist, along with a handful of explosives and a device she called a "destabilizer" that would knock men off their feet.

"There's all kinds of security," said Will. "Once we get in, how will we get out?"

"Leave that to me," said Sula.

She led us through a maze of corridors as if she knew them by heart. Up an emergency stairwell to the sub-levels. From there another corridor to the deeper recesses of the blue octagon. As we walked we could hear the machines: constant and deep, a low pulsing that thrummed in my bones. The stairs and handrail vibrated, and the dirty yellow lights flickered and blinked. Sula walked with grim determination, like a woman returning to the scene of a crime. Will limped as he followed her. I tried to keep my mind off the pain in my shoulder by recalling the color of the sheets in my bedroom, the way the floor creaked when our father rose in the morning, the smell of my mother's hair when she unclipped it from her barrette and let it fan across the pillows.

Finally we emerged into the gloom of sub-level three. There was hardly any light except for what filtered through the poorly riveted walls and the glow cast from two sodium lamps at either end of a narrow hallway. The smell was loathsome, as if the ocean had coughed up its dead and decayed, then retreated. I could barely breathe. Will stumbled but grabbed the wall and held himself upright.

Sula raised one hand, signaling quiet.

We listened, but the only sounds were the familiar ones of pylons creaking in the tide, the rattling of rusty metal, and the ever-present drone of seawater under pressure, turning dross into gold.

"Why is it so quiet?" I whispered.

Sula shook her head.

Perhaps everyone was asleep or unconscious. Maybe the prisoners had been moved. Or maybe there were no longer any prisoners. Maybe the bodies had been dumped into the ocean to decompose and disappear.

Our eyes adjusted, and then we could see a single light leaking from beneath a closed door—the only sign of life, but at least it was something. Sula unclipped an explosive cap from her belt. "Stand clear," she commanded.

I nearly tripped as I backed into Will. He was holding on to a steel box that protruded from the wall. We barely had enough time to cover our faces when the cap blew, spewing smoke and steel into the corridor. The door swung open, spilling light into the hallway. Plastene and metal flakes filled the air, twirling, sparkling, then settling into darkness.

Sula advanced cautiously, hand on her harpoon. I trailed two steps behind. We stepped gingerly around the strewn metal, over the fallen door, and into the yawning opening of the cramped torture chamber.

There, facing us, gun drawn, sat Nasri.

"Welcome," he said. Then the lights went out.

CHAPTER 18

I was never certain which came first: the gunshot or the scream. My head hit the floor, and all was still. In the darkness there was only the blur of motion—faint outlines and shadowy imagination. In that split second between vision and nothingness, I couldn't distinguish between the two. Was I injured? Was I dead? I was surprised by how peaceful I felt, how tranquil and serene. I lay on the floor, and all was preternaturally calm, as in the moments before a sandstorm. It was Sula's voice that awakened me from my reverie. "Vera? Vera?"

So I was not dead. Or perhaps we both were.

Then the lights flickered on. Nasri's chair had tipped over. The harpoon jutted from his chest. His lips were peeled back in a deathly grimace, and his eyes were fixed open. He looked like a man who did not expect to die and had left the earth as he had emerged: howling in agony.

Sula stood over me. "You're bleeding," she said.

I felt my face. My hands came away sticky. A great lump rose up in my throat, and my breath caught on something hard. "I've been shot?" It was a question more than a statement, because I didn't feel wounded—although I had begun to feel cold and shaky.

"Sit tight," Sula commanded. Her hands were in my hair, then on my head, pressing and probing. I tried hard not to panic, but the top of my head burned, and my forehead was wet with slickness.

Will stopped short when he saw me. "Vera?" he began, but could not finish. He looked to Sula for reassurance, but she was too busy examining me. There was nothing he could do but take my hand.

A bullet had grazed my scalp, Sula concluded. It had cleared a tiny path like a trail through the geno-soy fields and burned off the top layer of skin. A flesh wound, literally, but it bled like something worse. Sula tore off a sleeve from my shirt and bandaged it as best she could.

"It's not pretty," she said. "The scalp bleeds the worst. But it's nothing to worry about. When it heals, you won't even know it was there."

I tried to smile but feared I would cry. "I always wondered what it was like to be shot."

"Now you've lived to tell the tale."

I touched my scalp where Sula had wrapped the cloth. It still burned, but it made me feel important. I'd been wounded in combat. Anyone could break a leg or dislocate a shoulder, but how many people got shot? I could tell by the way Will was looking at me that he was impressed too and not a little bit jealous. I would have quickly traded the head wound, however, for a glass of clean water.

"Who shut off the light?" I asked.

"I threw the switch," Will said. He'd been leaning against a box that controlled power for the floor. He cut the voltage as soon as he'd heard Nasri's voice.

"Quick thinking," Sula remarked. She leaned over to pull the harpoon from Nasri's chest. I covered my eyes in the crook of Will's elbow.

"Where are they?" I asked, my voice muffled by Will's arm.

"Not here."

But Sula was wrong. A low moaning interrupted her efforts to retrieve the harpoon. In the dark corner of the small room—hard to believe we could miss it—a pile of blankets stirred. I ran over and tossed them aside.

"Ulysses!"

His face was battered and bruised; dried blood caked his beard; his trousers were sheared at the knees and crusted from his wound—but he was alive. His eyelids fluttered, but he couldn't open them. He tried to speak, but no words emerged.

I put my lips next to his ear. "It's okay," I whispered. "I'm here. We're going to take care of you."

I wasn't sure Ulysses understood me, but I kept repeating the words in the hope that he would.

Sula reached into a pouch on her belt and withdrew a syringe. I jumped to my feet and nearly grabbed it. "Adrenaline," she explained. "His body needs energy."

I tried to relax. I had to trust her, just as I'd trusted Ulysses. I helped Sula roll up Ulysses's sleeve. Then Sula injected him. Nothing happened at first, but in a few moments he stirred, then moved his head and opened his eyes. They fixed on Sula.

"Who are you?" he asked gruffly.

"She's Sula," I said, stroking Ulysses's bearded cheek.

"Where are we?"

I explained that we were still inside Bluewater. We had rescued him from the torture chamber, and Nasri was dead. "Sula knows how to escape." I turned to her. "Don't you?" I asked.

"Getting in is easy," said Sula. "Getting out will be more difficult. If they see us boarding the skimmer, they'll catch us. The boat is slower than anything they've got."

"So we can't let them see us," I said.

"We'll need to take out their eyes." Her smile was lined and hard, but, like Ulysses's, hid mischief.

I nodded.

"It won't work," Will said. "They'll catch us on the beach. We need something faster."

"Yes, and it'd be nice to have some commandos while we're dreaming," Sula muttered.

"You said you could drive anything," Will continued. "They have jets."

Sula's eyes brightened.

"They'll never expect it," he went on.

"But we can't leave Kai here," I protested.

Sula frowned. "Who said anything about leaving without him? He's worth too much to leave behind."

"You're not going to sell him!" I said, horrified.

"Sell him? Do I look like a merc?"

I hesitated. But her violet eyes made me trust her. Whatever suffering she'd endured had made her unblinking and resolute.

We helped Ulysses to his feet. He was weak, but the adrenaline helped. Sula quickly examined him and confirmed nothing was broken.

"I could have told you that," Ulysses growled.

"Oh, Ulysses, she's just worried about you." For the first time since we had left home, I felt a surge of optimism. Our group of three had grown to four, and soon, I hoped, we would be six.

Sula led us out of the cell into the dim hallway. "So you're the great pirate king?" she asked.

"Not a king," he said. "I've explained that."

"I always wondered what pirates did with all that water they stole."

"We don't *steal* water. We take it from people who don't deserve it."

"Ah, you mean from the pipelines that irrigate crops for innocent children?"

"And I suppose you deliver the water you're skimming from this abomination to orphans and widows?"

They bickered like this for a while, but I could tell they admired each other. Two fighters; two survivors. Sula, the loner. Ulysses, the leader. Where she was impulsive, he was measured and deliberate. Where she would strike first, he would strike back. Their differences, however, were less important than their common enemy: Bluewater.

"The boy will be in the presentation room," said Ulysses.

Sula put her hand on her harpoon. "We'll need more weapons."

"I don't care how quick you are with that spear, you'll not outfight the security forces of a half-dozen nations."

"I've fought twenty men and killed them all."

"Were they armed?"

"Of course they were armed!"

"Listen to me. You'll not beat these people by killing them. For every one you kill, there will be two more coming at you. And what about the children? What do you plan to do with them? Give them weapons?"

"I can fire a gun," said Will.

Sula turned to him as if she might consider it, then she swung back to Ulysses. "You have a better idea?"

"We'll need a distraction.

"Such as?"

"Bluewater needs water. What if it were dammed?"

"That's impossible."

"Easier than killing hundreds."

Sula was not a listener, but she remained silent while Ulysses outlined his plan. Soon she was nodding while Ulysses scratched a rough schematic in the dust.

"It will be a race to get out of here," he concluded, "You'll have to prepare the skimmer for all of us."

"Sula can fly jets," said Will.

Ulysses stared at her with newfound admiration. "Bluewater has jets."

"What was your first clue?" asked Sula as if she were talking to an infant.

I watched Ulysses recalibrate this information. His brow furrowed, and the bird tattooed on his neck dipped its wing. "The jetport will have a security detail."

"They'll be looking for us on the water," said Sula.

"It won't take long for them to figure out their mistake."

"I'll need five minutes."

Ulysses nodded. I knew that pirates worked together, their groups small but well-coordinated. I surveyed our group. Two of us had never handled a weapon, three of us were injured, and the four of us were badly outnumbered. Yet our survival—and Kai's—depended on our collective effort. Ulysses divvied up the tasks. Sula and I would cause the diversion. Ulysses and Will would make their way to the presentation room. If everything went as planned, we would meet on the roof, where the jets were parked.

"Be careful," Ulysses instructed. "Stay low, and keep to the corners. Avoid the open halls. If there's shooting, don't engage; keep moving."

"You be careful too," I said to him. The drug Sula had given him was wearing off, and he flinched when I took his hand. His skin was sallow. Beads of perspiration lined his forehead. But his grip was strong, and his eyes were focused and intense. He pulled me closer, and his warm body and pirate smell enveloped me: wood smoke and sand.

"After this, no matter what happens, no more rescues," he said softly to my ear. "Promise me that."

I nodded solemnly. If we didn't rescue Kai, there wasn't going to be a second chance. We would never see our parents again.

As if he sensed my fear, Ulysses said, "I'll get you home. Word of honor."

"No one's going home if we don't hurry," said Sula. I gave Will a hug, but there was no time to linger. Sula moved swiftly for the stairwell, and I hurried to catch up.

The steel steps glistened, but rust had already begun to wear through on the risers. Like everything else about Bluewater, the shiny surfaces hid corrosion and corruption. The entire edifice was a monument to ignorance. The truth was that butterflies could not disrupt an entire ecosystem simply by beating their wings. It took willful neglect and deliberate blindness, the refusal to see the obvious even as the land grew toxic before our eyes. But I still held out hope that we could change our ways.

"How far?" I gasped.

"Sea room," she said. "Lowest level."

Ulysses had taken Nasri's gun; Sula had scavenged his knife and laser-taser. As we walked she showed me how to use the laser, aiming its precise beam at any large muscle group but avoiding the head, where it could incapacitate an enemy. "Legs, stomach, or groin," she said. "Shoot first, then ask your questions."

I couldn't imagine shooting a man, but I knew it might be possible. At least the laser-taser wouldn't kill anyone. I hoped Sula wouldn't either.

We went down the stairwell, back in the direction from which we had climbed. The drone of the desalinating machinery was like the advancing rumble of a convoy. Sula was explaining how much power desalination required, but by the time we reached the double safety doors, I could barely hear a word she was saying.

The doors were bolted, but Sula blew them easily with an explosive cap. Bluewater's defenses were directed outward: toward the coast and the ragtag boats that troubled its boundaries. Frontal attack, not sabotage, was its main concern.

Inside, the sea room was louder than jet engines. Five enormous pipes sucked in water and transported it to steel cisterns. But much worse than the noise was the smell. Foul, rank, and fetid—tons of seaweed and other waste rotted in giant holding tanks from which they would eventually be dumped back into the ocean. Sula knew that the waste had to be cleared from screens inside the pipes twice daily, or else they would clog, and the desalination process would grind to a halt.

We had no gloves or masks. Sula fashioned them as best she could from the remaining cloth of my shirt's sleeves and her own wet suit. But they were clumsy, and soon both of us were scooping rotting seaweed from the containers with our bare hands. At first I nearly passed out from the stink. Then when I grew used to the odor, my hands burned from the chemicals. My eyes filled with tears, and the back of my throat felt as if someone had scratched it raw.

We removed the filtering screens from the intake pipes easily enough. But stuffing them with rotten seaweed required pressing the debris into the tiny mesh so that it would not fall out. A foul brown liquid seeped between our fingers, and my hands were red and blistered before we had even completed one screen.

We worked as if in a fever, horrific fumes filling our lungs, our bodies clammy and wet. At any moment we expected the guards to burst in, and Sula's hand was never too far from her harpoon. Seawater roared through the pipes as we packed each screen with garbage. The floor of the sea room was slick with slime. Each step grew more treacherous, each breath more perilous.

When the five screens were packed with garbage, and Sula had made certain no liquid could leak through, we lifted the first screen gently so as not to dislodge the seaweed. Then we tried to slide it back into its slot as seawater rushed madly about our hands. It slipped in easily at first, but jammed near the end as the water pressure grew. I tried to help shove it in, but my bad shoulder made it impossible to push on anything. Even my good shoulder hurt when I tried pushing with that arm. But Sula's strength made up for my weakness. The muscles in her forearms knotted and bulged as she shoved the screen with all her might and forced it to lock into place.

The remaining screens were easier. With each one we improved on the angle. I discovered that if we lifted the screen several millimeters off its track, it slid in with less resistance. One by one we shut down the intake of water from the ocean until the pipes were completely blocked and the holding tanks were emptied.

The sound of the clogged water was unlike anything on this Earth: a low keening, like some prehistoric animal bellowing in its death throes. Without the polluted sea to process, the pumps sucked nothing but air, creating a vacuum in the pipes that strained and threatened to buckle them.

But the pumps had been constructed to handle just such an emergency. After twenty seconds an alarm sounded, and the machinery shut down. Strobe lights flashed. A recorded voice blared warnings through amplified speakers. To compensate for the loss in pressure, steam blasted through the pipes, leaking from cracks in the fittings and spilling into the room like smoke.

Sula grabbed my hand and pulled me toward the doors. We

raced for the stairs even as we could hear voices shouting nearby. There was no going down. The only direction was up. We took two steps at a time, tripping but not falling, running as fast as we could manage. The flashing lights made it seem as if we were in a holo-cast: flickering images and half-seen pursuers in the iridescent blackness.

Sula's hand went to the harpoon. She held it above her head as she pushed me ahead of her on the stairs.

That's when I heard the staccato burst of gunfire and felt the pulse of concussion grenades. They were close—plaster rained from the ceiling, and the walls exploded. Then my feet left the ground, and I was falling down, down, down…

CHAPTER 19

I landed hard on my back. Grit blanketed my lips and eyes. My neck ached, and there was a lump on my skull. Sula lay beside me, one arm cradling my head. I tried to sit up, but she stopped me. "Stay put," she ordered.

We had fallen two floors. Bullets ricocheted above us like angry sand hornets. Below us all was silent.

"Who's shooting?" I whispered.

"Stop talking," she hissed.

The alarms continued to sound. Emergency lights cast a yellow glow, while strobes flashed intermittently. While we lay in the semi-darkness, hidden behind the broken wall, six black-booted men thumped past us in stairwell. I folded myself into Sula, burying my head in her ribs. Stray wisps of blond hair brushed my face. Her sea-soap smell was in my mouth. My head rose on the sharp intake of her breath. Then the men passed.

We waited behind the wall until Sula was certain it was safe. In the sea room the men had probably found the clogged screens and were working to clean them. We could only hope the distraction served its purpose. While Bluewater guards rushed to contain the damage, Ulysses and Will gained precious minutes to get to the presentation room. But the gunfire meant something had gone wrong. Bluewater should have been hunting for Sula and me below, not Will and Ulysses above.

Sula pushed me into the dusty hall and then onto the staircase. The walls were blown away, but the stairs were intact. We stepped over broken glass, plaster chunks, even a dead body—a guard, face down. We did not slow.

The octagon fortress was not nearly as tall as it was wide. I realized now that it covered the sea floor and was barely visible from the shoreline. Anyone searching for two escaped fugitives would have a lot of ground to cover. They would naturally start near the water, where the sea room was located and the skimmer was docked: the most logical place to escape. The roof was the last place they would think to look.

That's why the two guards on the roof were more surprised than we were to see a young girl and a woman in a wet suit. Their hesitation was the only advantage Sula needed. She swiftly killed one man with her harpoon and knocked the other unconscious with a blow to the back of his head.

"Did you have to kill him?" I protested.

Sula retrieved her weapon. "What would you like me to do? Give him a kiss?"

"Why can't you use the destabilizer? Or the taser?"

"In the time it takes to knock him out, his friend pulls a gun on me—and you."

I didn't say anything, but it seemed to me that Sula preferred to kill people, as if she were harboring a grudge she could never pay back. "What did they do to you here?" I asked.

"What didn't they do?"

"But you're alive."

Sula stopped cleaning the harpoon and regarded me for a minute. Then she slowly pulled her wet suit away from her shoulder to reveal an ugly scar that ran beneath her collarbone and across her entire chest. It was purple and red, knotted and lumpy. It looked as if the skin had been ripped rather than cut. It had obviously bled for a long time and never been stitched or cared for properly. Whoever had injured her had wanted it to hurt.

The wet suit snapped angrily as it fell back into place.

"They called it a *lesson*," she said. "But they should have found a better student."

I looked away, out to the flat gray expanse of the sea. Bluewater operated in a lawless vacuum. Governments—even the worst of them—had to answer to the people. History had proved that even the most brutal dictatorships collapsed. Wasn't that what we'd learned in school, that Illinowa had to answer to its citizens? But to whom did Bluewater answer?

We were adjacent to the runway but sheltered behind the emergency stairwell. We could see two jets and three helicopters. A platoon of soldiers guarded the planes, but they seemed distracted and bored. They were not yet missing their two dead comrades. Alarms still rang on the lower floors, although no one had fired a shot for a while. There was no sign of Ulysses or Will.

"Where are they?" I asked.

"They'll come."

I wished I felt as confident as Sula. I told myself that Ulysses would protect Will. The pirate king had survived many scraps and scrapes, but surely nothing compared to infiltrating Bluewater's global headquarters. He had his wits and Nasri's gun and a shot of adrenaline that was wearing off. I hoped it would be enough.

Then they appeared. Ulysses looked gray and weathered, while Will was flushed and breathing hard. But they were alone.

"Where's Kai?" I cried.

"Everyone fled when the shooting started," Ulysses answered.

"Why didn't you hold your fire?" Sula asked.

Ulysses growled at her. "It wasn't *our* shooting. Their cozy little meeting broke up in gunfire."

Sula's eyebrows dipped and knitted as she tried to register this information. "Who was shooting?"

Ulysses explained that before they had reached the presentation room, they'd heard a loud argument and then gunshots.

"Put a damper on the rest of the gathering," he concluded.

"We might have gotten in too," said Will. "But everyone scattered."

"What could they be fighting about?" I asked.

"What they always fight about," said Ulysses. "The future and who'll control it."

"It's bedlam now," said Sula.

"This'll suit our purposes," said Ulysses. "When everyone's running, they have to run somewhere."

"It's the direction I'm worried about," said Sula.

"Patience."

I didn't know how Ulysses could urge patience when things had gone so disastrously wrong. If the politicians were shooting at each other,

Kai and his father were trapped. And when the shooting stopped, surely someone would spirit them away, making rescue impossible.

But patience wasn't necessary. The emergency doors on the far edge of the roof burst open, and a handful of guards emerged, leading a man who was nearly a head taller than any of them and a boy who was paler and thinner since the last time I saw him. My chest tightened.

"*Hello,*" Ulysses whispered. He crouched low and thrust out an arm to prevent Sula from rising. "We have guests."

With all the shooting below, I could see now that the roof was the most logical escape route for Torq and his men. The guards were on high alert, and they moved cautiously, with guns extended and fingers on the triggers. Kai and his father were not cuffed or bound, but Torq grasped the father's wrist in his hand. Next to Kai's father, Torq didn't look quite so tall, but he still outweighed the man by twenty kilos. Torq's brown hairless body was shining like a genetically modified fruit—built to withstand drought, disease, and predators.

"There's fifteen rounds in that chamber," said Sula, nodding at Ulysses's gun, "and I can take two before they even start shooting."

"The gun's half-empty," Ulysses responded. "And there's a dozen guards on the roof besides the men with baldy."

Sula scratched a tooth with the tip of one finger. "Once they're on that jet, there's no way to catch them."

"They won't get on the jet."

I crawled to Will's side and whispered in his ear. "Kai looks just like his father."

It was true: Driesen Smith was a more elongated version of the boy. Both were tall with blond hair and had the same way of standing, as if nothing were important, even as their lives were in the hands of corporate criminals. But Driesen glanced surreptitiously about the roof, and I could tell he was deciding whether there might still be an escape. A driller didn't survive for long without being skilled at seizing opportunity where others wouldn't dare.

They were probably less than a hundred meters away, yet the distance was nearly insurmountable. I wanted to wave to Kai, to tell him we had come to save him, but he was barely visible behind a phalanx of soldiers. A few steps, a quick dash, and I could pull Kai away, but I would never make it half that distance alive.

As my stomach churned and the air filled with the crackling static of communicators, an idea came to me. It was simple, really—not dangerous at all—but I had to convince Ulysses and Sula to let me try.

"I'm going to get him," I said.

"Don't be crazy," said Will.

"I can do it. I'll take the destabilizer."

Sula shook her head. "No. If anyone takes it, I will."

"They'll shoot you before you get close enough," I said. "They know you're armed. I'm the only one who can get inside and use it."

I knew I was right, and I knew the others knew it as well. But Will refused to hear me. "I'll do it," he said. "They won't shoot me."

"You're too old. They'll think you're a soldier, and they won't let you get near."

In normal circumstances Will might have been flattered to be considered a soldier. But the only way to walk unarmed into the midst of Bluewater's elite security force was to appear harmless and nonthreatening. I was the only one with that chance.

"We can intercept them at the plane," Will offered.

"It'll be too late by then."

He turned to Ulysses. "Don't let her do it."

"I want to," I insisted. "Kai is my friend. It was my idea to come after him in the first place. Besides, I'll be fine."

Ulysses frowned, but his eyes betrayed him. "She's the only one who can slip past unchallenged," he agreed. "It's our best chance." Will wanted to argue, but the decision was already made. "If there's any sign of trouble," said Ulysses, "dive to the floor, and don't come up until the shooting stops."

Sula handed me the destabilizer. It was no larger than a bottle cap, and she strapped it to my wrist like a timepiece. She explained that when I pushed two small protruding buttons at the same time, it would generate a shock wave that would knock down anyone within a ten-meter radius. "But make sure you stand straight and have both feet on the ground, or it will take you with it," she added.

I ran my fingers over its smooth black surface. I was amazed that such a small device had so much power. But there was only enough charge for one shock wave, so I would have just one chance. Sula gripped my arm as if she was going to say something more, but all she said was, "Hurry now."

I hugged Ulysses and Will. Will gave me one last chance to change my mind, then made me promise I wouldn't take any foolish risks.

"At least none you wouldn't," I said. Despite himself, he grinned back at me.

I stole one last look at the destabilizer, memorizing the location of the buttons, then I stepped from the hiding place out into the open. The guards turned to me in surprise, as if they had just seen a phantom.

"Kai!" I waved.

Sights raised, the guns bristled at me. I held my breath.

"Vera?" Kai's face was as confused as the men's around him.

The gun of the leading guard lowered slightly, and the man peered at me over his barrel. "Identify yourself!" he called.

"I'm a friend of Kai's," I said.

"The pirate's daughter." Torq pushed to the front of the group, his brown head glistening in the sun. "But where is your father? He can't have gotten far."

"You have him in your prison."

"He's gone. But I think you know that." He turned to the nearest guard. "Search her."

One of the guards swiftly approached and checked me for weapons, but he was young and nervous, and I could tell he felt uncomfortable running his hands over my body. He didn't even think to inspect the timepiece on my wrist. The other guards lowered their guns. I'm sure they didn't think I posed any threat. Torq signaled to two of them, and they escorted me back inside their circle.

"Hi, Kai," I said, as if we were meeting on the road after school again.

"Hi, Vera."

We grinned at each other like idiots. I couldn't have been happier if someone had handed me a real orange with a glass of fresh water.

"This is not a game," said Torq. "Whatever your father's planned, it won't succeed. We'll be in the air before he or anyone else can stop us."

The circle of guards pressed more tightly around me. Torq gave them their orders, and they marched us toward three waiting helicopters.

"Where are you going?" I asked.

"Silence!" thundered Torq.

My right hand touched my left wrist. I felt strangely calm. Even though I was surrounded, I felt no fear. "It's going to be okay," I said to Kai. "We're here to rescue you."

Torq turned to me at that moment, his arm raised as if to strike. His sudden motion caused me to stumble slightly backward, so that when I pressed the buttons on the destabilizer, my left foot was barely touching the ground. I felt a blow to my solar plexus like someone had tossed a hundred-kilo bag of sand at my stomach. My vision went wobbly, the way a wi-cast lost its rectangular shape and became blobbish when the transmission was interrupted. At first I didn't even see the men crumpling around me, falling like their bones were broken. My feet went out from under me, and I collapsed too.

I was barely conscious when Ulysses lifted me to his shoulder and carried me at a full run toward the jets. This was a man with a piece of metal in his upper thigh, several cracked ribs, and contusions across his back and neck. But he ran like a pan-republic champion, hunched low and aerodynamic, his body shielding me while he emptied Nasri's gun at the phalanx of guards by the runway. At his side Sula loosed a volley of harpoons while she kept Will safely behind her.

Although outnumbered, Ulysses and Sula had the advantage of surprise, speed, and deadly accuracy. The guards were soft from a life of easy water, while Ulysses and Sula were tempered by hardship and thirst. A half-dozen men were dead or wounded before the remaining guards even knew they were being attacked. The others scattered quickly, and only a few managed to return fire before they were shot down. One guard blocked the doorway to the nearest jet, but Sula quickly felled him with a second knife she kept sheathed at her ankle. Another guard stepped from behind a walkway, but Ulysses knocked him unconscious with the butt of the gun.

All this happened in a flash. The images of violence, explosions, and scattered gunshots barely registered. Later Will filled in the missing details. I was alert enough, however, to realize that we had left Kai and his father with Torq and his men.

"Kai!" I cried.

"We're not done yet," growled Ulysses.

Torq and his men twitched on the ground, but Sula had already climbed into the cockpit of the jet and started the engines. Ulysses lay me down in the small compartment meant for the pilot's gear, and Will squeezed in next to me. Then Ulysses climbed into the copilot's seat. The plane shook violently as Sula increased the power to the engines.

"You sure you know how to fly one of these?" Ulysses asked.

Sula glared at him. "Sure you know how to fasten your seat belt?"

The ping of bullets striking the wings cut short their spat. One hit the windshield, leaving an irregular star on the glass. Ulysses pulled the safety strap across his shoulder and buckled himself into his seat.

Sula maneuvered the jet across the runway. The engines roared loudly as she increased the thrust. Outside Torq had risen unsteadily to his feet; I could see him shouting orders at his men. Sula drove the plane directly toward him, accelerating quickly as his men scrambled for their weapons. She could have mowed them down or fired a rocket into their midst, but Kai was still unconscious on the ground, and his father stood shakily over him.

The end of the runway was just one hundred meters distant. Sula braked and swung the jet around. The engines sprayed hot exhaust at Torq and his men, and they dropped to the ground to avoid the burning fuel. Sula kept the engines roaring at full blast. The inferno of gas set the roof ablaze. "Thirty seconds," she said to Ulysses.

"You better cover me." He unlatched the door.

"I'm wasting fuel," said Sula.

"I'm not kidding." He stepped from the plane onto the concrete runway. The air crinkled around him, hot and dry, all the oxygen burned out of it. There was no way he could breathe in the heat. But he hunkered low and ran for the soldiers, as if he might try to take them all at once. The men struggled to grasp their weapons. Their arms tensed and flexed as they tried to make their muscles respond in their weakened state.

Driesen Smith rose to one knee, while Kai remained unconscious. Ulysses reached the father and slung the boy over one shoulder. Driesen could barely move, so Ulysses lifted him with one arm and half-dragged, half-carried him across the runway. The guards shouted for him to stop, but they couldn't manage to squeeze off any shots. Several tried to run after him, staggering and weaving, buckling and then rising again. But Ulysses kept going, relentless and indestructible. At the door of the jet, Driesen Smith hesitated. His long blond lashes fluttered rapidly, and his jaw hung open. He seemed to be weighing the risks of jumping into a plane with a crazed pirate against staying on the ground with corporate assassins. Probable death versus certain death.

"Move it!" Ulysses yelled and tossed him in the jet like a sack of dry-crete. Then he tossed Kai on top of him.

"Careful!" I said.

"No time for careful. Fly," Ulysses commanded.

Sula didn't hesitate. She threw the engines into gear and blasted toward the edge of the runway. Bullets sang out harmlessly in the vapor trail behind us. In a moment we were airborne, with only the ocean and the sky between us and home.

CHAPTER 20

We flew fast and silently. With our faces pressed to the window, we could barely feel the vibration from the powerful engines. Thin wisps of clouds spidered below us, delicate and fragile. The glass was cold to our cheeks. Inside the temperature dropped rapidly, but at least we had oxygen and blankets. Sula explained we were traveling at nearly twice the speed of sound, beyond the barrier where words could catch us.

"We're safe—for now," she added.

Kai leaned against me, conscious but unable to speak. His head rested on my shoulder. I glanced at his father, whose left arm hung useless at his side. Sula told us it could be several hours before the effects of the destabilizer completely wore off.

"Sula rescued us from the fortress," I told Kai. "And Ulysses saved us from the mines."

"You escaped from the fortress on your own," said Sula.

"And it was you who saved me from Bluewater," said Ulysses.

"But we never could have rescued them without your help," I said.

I told Kai the entire story then: about finding Martin the bodyguard dead and Kai's insulin abandoned in the bath, about following the clues to the old well, about traveling with the pirates to the dam, being captured by PELA, escaping, and then falling into the hands of Bluewater.

"But now we're safe," I said. "And soon we'll be home."

Kai squeezed my hand.

"They'll come after you," said Driesen—his first words since boarding the jet.

"Ha! I'd like to see Torq show his face in Basin," said Ulysses.

"Bluewater *owns* Basin," said Driesen.

"A company can't own a city," I said.

Driesen grimaced. "You're just a child. You don't know anything about the world. Bluewater owns the water; it owns the land; it owns the cities and republics."

"It doesn't own Canada," I protested.

"It owns the people who own Canada."

"And what about the war?"

"This war is nothing. An inconvenience."

I assumed Driesen was joking. I had seen the jets screaming across the sky and the tanks lumbering north. I had witnessed the boys who returned from the front lines with limbs missing, minds gone. The war was not an inconvenience. It was a shroud that covered the sun. It darkened our lives like the dust that settled on our hands and lips, making everything we tasted and touched dry, bitter, and fruitless.

"There's a bigger war about to happen," Driesen continued. "A world war. These other wars are skirmishes, police actions. Fights over borders and boundaries. But soon there will only be two sides:

people with water, and those without. The next battle—the final battle—will be about who controls the spigot."

"And Bluewater?" I asked.

"It plays both sides. But it needs a sponsor to protect its operations. So it aligns itself with the water-powerful and keeps knowledge of new supplies from the waterless."

No one spoke. What Driesen said made sense. The republics' water started in Canada, and the Canadians' water started in the Arctic, and the Arctic's water started as rain from the clouds. But the Canadians had dammed the rivers, the Europeans had drained the polar cap, and the Chinese had sucked the storm clouds from the sky. To survive it was not enough to hoard water; it had to be stolen from one's enemies. Small wars turned into larger wars, and the large wars would become one war. If the Canadians weren't fighting the Australians yet, it was just a matter of time.

"We have to stop them," I said.

"You can't defeat them," said Driesen. "They have too much money and too many resources."

"But we have Kai!" I said.

"And they won't stop until they have him back."

"How can you say that about your son?"

Driesen grimaced again. "Don't you think I've tried to protect him? I've done everything I could. Hired bodyguards. Disguised our identities. Made secret deals with other republics. But Bluewater is different. What it doesn't own, it buys."

"Kai said there was a river."

Driesen's laugh was like a half-formed cough. "There is *no* river."

I looked at him but saw nothing funny. Kai raised his head from my shoulder, as if he wanted to say something but he didn't have the strength.

"Kai said he would take me there."

"That was just a story."

"A story?" I managed.

"We told it to keep people away."

"From what?"

The jet banked hard, and my stomach rose into my chest. Kai clenched my arm, and at first I thought he was frightened; then I realized he was holding me because he thought *I* was.

"Idiots are shooting at us," said Sula.

Hundred of tracer bullets lit the sky around the jet. I peered out the window. We were thousands of meters above a ruined city that was no doubt controlled by vigilantes or mercenaries. A downed jet would be a real prize, its captured crew a treasure in ransom. Sula banked hard again, then climbed swiftly. The tracers disappeared, and my stomach settled. Kai let go of my arm; his fingers left fine red marks on my skin.

Driesen was watching as Kai settled back against my shoulder. Then his expression softened, and he looked merely quizzical. "We were drilling for water in a virgin aquifer," he said.

"The aquifers have all been tapped," said Ulysses gruffly.

"No," said Driesen. "Not all of them. There's confined aquifers sit below a surface aquifer. Men drain the water they see but don't realize there's more water below. It takes real skill to find the water. It takes a gift—like Rikkai's."

"And where *is* this geological marvel?" Ulysses demanded. He sounded as if he thought Driesen's tale was just driller hocus-pocus. Drillers were notorious for their tall tales and dreams of wealth. Yet most died without a credit chip to their names.

"It can only be reached with special drilling equipment that Tinker and I developed. But there's water, billions of liters, never been touched. More than enough for all of Illinowa."

Could it be? It was as if Driesen had said there were diamonds, free for the taking, polished and cut, gleaming in a pile like tomorrow's promise. Everyone in that plane was silent, imagining the riches.

Kai's lips were chapped and cracked, and his voice was harsh and raspy. He lifted his head and looked at me. "Water," he said. "To start again."

With all the talk about aquifers, we had forgotten that Kai and Driesen might be thirsty. I grabbed Sula's canteen and helped Kai drink a long mouthful. Then I gave the rest to his father. I recalled that Kai had told me the symptoms of his diabetes began with a great thirst, a desire for water he couldn't quench. It was as if his disease became his gift, his illness the cure for all of our sickness.

"We'll need that equipment," said Ulysses.

"It's still at the dam PELA blew, I expect. Bluewater wasn't interested in the water. They just wanted Kai."

"Sula," said Ulysses.

"Give me the coordinates," she responded, and then she punched them into the onboard navigator.

"It's the first place they'll look," said Driesen.

"We'll not stay long enough for them to find us," she said.

"And then what?" Driesen said bitterly. "You'll have the entire Minnesota Water Guard looking for us. To say nothing of Bluewater."

Ulysses sniffed. "Maybe we'll just leave you at the dam."

"Ulysses!" I scolded him.

"Without me, you can't work the equipment," Driesen said. "Without Rikkai, you won't know where to drill."

"We're not leaving you anywhere," I said. "Ulysses is just cranky."

The pirate gritted his teeth. "You'd be cranky too if you had shrapnel in your hip."

"What good will it do?" asked Will. "The dam's in Minnesota. We'll never get the water home."

"The aquifer runs below most of the republic, and Minnesota too. It runs all the way up to Canada," said Driesen. "We were drilling in Minnesota, because that's where Tinker lived, and the barrier was shallow. We could drill right below Basin. But that won't solve your problem."

"Bluewater," I said.

"They won't let anyone drill," agreed Driesen. "We tried, and look what happened. They won't let anyone access free water if it threatens their hold."

"Unless they don't have a choice," I said.

"How so?" asked Ulysses.

"We make them an offer they can't refuse."

"Ha! You sound like a pirate now!"

I *felt* like a pirate, suddenly enthused by a wily and implausible plan. "Listen," I said.

The others fell silent as the jet flew northwest into the setting sun.

We had only one-third of a tank of fuel, but Sula said it would be enough. The jet could fly on one engine if needed, and the wind would do the rest. Driesen had everything he needed at the drilling site, I explained. We didn't need a lot of water, just enough to fill several cisterns. There were cameras everywhere, and it was only a short flight home. Torq and his men would find us—it was impossible to escape—but by then it would be too late. At least that was the plan.

"It's a good plan," Ulysses acknowledged.

More important, it was our only plan. Bluewater would surely never stop until it recaptured Kai, and the rest of us might be killed if we got in its way. We couldn't keep running. Not when we were so close to home.

"Vera?" Kai managed.

I leaned close to his lips.

He spoke with a deep rasp, but I could understand him. He told me then about the mercs who had come looking for them, the gun battle in which Martin was killed, how they had been forced to disclose Dr. Tinker's location. The mercs flew them to Bluewater, where Torq refused to give Kai insulin until Driesen revealed the site of the aquifer. Kai didn't know PELA had killed Dr. Tinker, and the news came as a blow. He and Driesen had worked together for years, and Kai considered him to be like an uncle.

"He could be crabby," said Kai, "but he was a good man."

I didn't disagree, although my memory of Dr. Tinker was less kind.

All the time in captivity, Kai said, he was thinking how to get a message to me. He said this without blushing, which only made me blush harder—especially because I could feel Will's eyes boring into me. Then Kai added, "The food was terrible. Not like your dad's guacamole."

I had to laugh that he would think about food at a time like this. But remembering my father's cooking made me miss it as well. There was a potato and soy cheese dish where the potato skins were crunchy and the cheese oozed from the top like caramel. There was another dish made of cactus and local grains that he cooked slowly for two days until it turned into a sweet pudding. My mouth watered at the memory of the meals, and I couldn't wait to dig into them again.

"Dad's going to be surprised," said Will. He tried to pretend he was brushing the hair from his eyes, but I could tell he was brushing away a tear.

For once I didn't feel like crying. I was too excited to tell our parents everything. In the safety of our home, our adventures would become like tall tales, hard to believe but fun to recount until truth and fiction became mashed together in one kaleido-scopic whole. I hugged Will and forgot all about the pain in my shoulder. It didn't matter, because soon I would have hours to lie on my bed.

We never saw the rocket. It exploded about five hundred meters in front of the left wing. The explosion shook the jet, sending us spiraling in a dangerous plunge until Sula regained control of the ailerons.

"Bluewater!" she cursed.

"I thought you left them behind."

"I was flying slower to conserve fuel. But looks like I miscalculated."

"Can we outrun them?" Will asked.

Sula shook her head. "No. They've got the same equipment we do. Hold on. It's going to be a dogfight."

The plane went into a steep dive. I screamed, although I didn't mean to. Kai gripped my arm. Will practically tumbled out of his seat. My ears popped and then popped again as I tried to gulp down oxygen. When it felt like the ride couldn't get any sicker, when we had fallen about as far as possible, Sula turned so we were actually upside down, hanging from our seat belts. For an instant we were weightless, floating in an air pocket. Then just as swiftly, gravity slammed us back into our seats. The plane groaned and vibrated madly. Kai moaned and held his stomach. I didn't feel much better.

"There may be worse to come," said Sula. She put the jet into a sharp bank left, then a hard bank right. Now we were behind the attacker. Somehow she had managed to flip on our pursuer by looping behind him. The other jet swirled and dipped, trying to shake us. It shrieked against the sky, then tore for the earth. Smoke spewed from its engines as the turbines worked at their highest thrust. But Sula dogged it like thread on a needle.

"Gotcha!" she whooped. She fired the rockets.

Two white lines burst from beneath the wings and raced across the blue. One exploded harmlessly behind the attacker's tail fin, but the other caught the rear stabilizer, which burst into flames. The jet shuddered and fluttered in the air like a butterfly. Then all at once, it exploded into a ball of fire.

"Heads down!" shouted Sula as we struck debris flying toward the windshield. Several large pieces slammed into the wing but none badly enough to crash us. Sula maintained control until we cleared the damage, then eased the plane to a lower altitude. Smoking bits of plastene and metal tumbled from the sky. But we were not safe—not yet.

"We've got trouble," said Sula when she reviewed the instrument panel. "You want the good news or the bad news?"

"Give us the bad first," said Ulysses.

"Even if we hadn't burned up most of our fuel in that dogfight, it seems we've punched a hole in the auxiliary tank."

"And the good news?"

"There is no good news."

The plane was vibrating severely now. Ominous red lights blinked on the control panel. I reached out for Will. "We'll be okay, right?" I asked.

"Sula can drive anything, remember?"

"Anything with an engine," said Sula. She was toggling the controls furiously, trying to maintain a level flight as the plane rapidly descended.

"There's a workable landing strip near the research lab," said Driesen. "They used it for copters, but it's long enough to land a plane."

She nodded, her eyes slits pinned to the ground below. "I can see it."

From the air the broken dam looked like a row of cracked teeth with the two largest ones missing. Water still spilled through the gap even though the Minnesotans had made an effort—with rubble and dirt—to close it. A flowing river was a strange sight, and it gave me a vision of the world in which my parents were born. It twisted and coursed, foaming white and brown, a thing alive and vibrant as it rushed uncontrolled toward the sea. Green vegetation had sprouted along its banks, like a holo of an ancient world.

"Hold on!" said Sula.

I tried to steady myself, but my breath came in quick short bursts and would not slow down. My nails dug into my palms, but I could barely feel the pain. I looked to Will. His face was as pale as I had ever seen it. Kai laid his hand on my forearm, but his fingertips trembled and moisture pearled his brow. There was nothing to do except put our faith in Sula and hang on.

The jet began to plummet. One moment I could see the low tops of buildings, the next moment we hit the ground hard enough to blow two tires. We screeched and veered off the runway, then careened through dirt and scrub at three hundred kilometers an hour, spinning crazily in a dust vortex. A window popped, and the door burst open. Sand, soot, and black smoke swirled into the plane. Someone was coughing, and someone else was yelling instructions. But somehow we slowed and came to a rest. "Everyone okay?" asked Sula.

We were, miraculously. No one was hurt, although my bad shoulder ached painfully where it had been restrained by the safety belt. Kai looked as if he might be sick, and Will's face had shaded from pale to green. Our stomachs settled as the air cleared.

Ulysses wasted no time in securing our position. He grabbed the laser-taser and his knife and pushed through the mangled door.

"Wait!" Sula shouted after him. "Men on the ground!"

It was too late. We heard the yelling. The roar of an engine. A

227

sound like a dog barking. Ulysses bellowed as if in great pain, and then his voice was buried. We braced for the onslaught.

I was outside before anyone could stop me. My feet touched ground, and my hands went up defensively, but I was knocked backward by something large and heavy. It sat on my chest and its hot breath washed over me.

I waited, eyes shut, for the jaws to clamp on my throat.

Cheetah barked, then licked my face again and again.

CHAPTER 21

We left Ulysses's men at the border.

The Minnesotans wouldn't let them cross without a bribe, and as Ulysses explained, the pirates had little to offer. They had lost ten men, much of their equipment, and Pooch in the flood. They needed to conserve resources for the next campaign. Besides, too many men would stir suspicion and cause a diversion before the job was done. Ulysses alone would come the rest of the way.

We took a truck, two sidearms, water for the journey, and Cheetah.

After all our travels, the trip south through Illinowa was like a Sunday jaunt. The roads were empty, and no one stopped or harassed us. Will and Kai slept most of the way, and I played Quarts with Sula while Cheetah rested on my lap. It was late afternoon by the time we arrived.

Torq found us at the gaming center. He appeared in a convoy of combat vehicles bristling with heavily armed men clad in black and blue. They surrounded the center and sealed access from the road. A bat-winged drone kept a lookout in the sky. Torq himself led a dozen gunmen through the doors. His shiny head gleamed in the artificial light, and his perfectly manicured hands caressed a machine pistol.

The gaming center was filled with the usual assortment of players. Boys and girls gathered at the consoles, competing for high scores and each other's attention while solitary men fed their chips into credit readers. On the walls, the screens broadcast a constant stream of content from across the globe: song and dance routines from YouToo!, news reports and info oddities in obscure languages— anything to distract people from their misery. The popular clips rose to the top, while the disfavored sank without a trace. The wireless was truly the most democratic forum in the world. Governments tried to filter it, but the signal could not be stopped. Any user with an uploader and a transmitter could post anything for the world to see: truth and lies in equal measure.

Torq couldn't kill us in the open. Not even he was brazen enough to shoot three people in plain view of a crowd. Besides, although his men were well-equipped and protected by kev-armor, it would have been a close battle against Ulysses and Sula. Torq told us to line up at the wall, but Ulysses refused, and Sula stepped in front of me.

"There'll be no heroes here," said Torq.

"Killing you wouldn't be heroic," said Sula.

Torq smiled, but his gray-blue eyes slitted black. "Where's the boy?"

"What boy?"

The sound of his safety catch clicked loudly.

"Put your weapon down," said Ulysses.

"A shame to have to kill the girl." His gun pointed at Sula, but I knew that when the shooting started, the bullets would go right through her.

Three boys playing Death Racer inched toward the walls, out of the line of fire. Two girls at Geyser let the imaginary water spray harmlessly while they ducked behind a pillar. They were old enough to know when to run.

"Not even Bluewater can cover up a massacre of innocents," said Ulysses.

"Don't be too sure," Torq said.

I held my breath. My plan had been a good one, but it required just a few more seconds. If the shooting started now, it would all be ruined. I stepped out from behind Sula.

"He's back there," I said, indicating the wi-booth behind us. "I'll get him."

I moved toward the booth before Torq called out to me, as I knew he would. "Stop!"

I stopped, turned slowly.

"Yes?" I asked politely, as if I were still innocent.

"I'm not a fool. Do you think I believe you'd just lead me to him? Come back here."

I walked as slowly as I could. Each step was excruciating, drawn out, as slow as I could make it. Naturally Torq thought I was frightened of him—he was so powerful with his weapons and muscles! And of course he didn't trust me—not after my trick with the destabilizer. I shuffled the last few steps, sliding awkwardly across the hard floor. When I was close, he reached out and grasped my wrist, then twisted my arm behind my back. I cringed and stifled a cry. The pain in my shoulder was unbearable. Ulysses started but stopped when Torq pressed his gun against my skull.

"Now," he said, face so close I could smell his skin. "Where is he?"

"In the booth," I managed.

"This is your last chance."

I didn't want to die, but if it gave us the time we needed, I was not afraid. The irony of being killed when we were so close to home was wretched, but there was a certain perverse logic to ending at the beginning. I let the moment linger as long as I could, each second improving our odds. Then I said, "It's the truth."

Before Torq could fire a shot, Kai emerged from the wi-booth, followed by Will and Driesen, as if they had been making a dance holo or posting wi-texts for everyone to see. They sauntered toward us. Torq released my wrist and pounced on Kai, who didn't resist. Ulysses grabbed me and clutched me to his side like his own daughter.

"This one's coming with me," Torq said to his men. "You can do what you want with the others."

"It's over," said Ulysses.

"Save your regrets for later."

"Look up."

At first one of the wi-screens seemed to be displaying a bad home holo: sand, dust, and machinery. But as the camera zoomed in, the image came into clearer view: A blue stream like life itself, shimmering with luminous clarity.

Water! It arced from the ground into the sky like the most extravagant fountain. It was Kai's secret river, unleashed from the earth and sharing its bounty with the land. Water fell from the heavens like an impossible storm. It soaked the dry beds, washed over desert scrub, and covered the dirt with water. It rained and rained, not for forty days and forty nights but long enough to make men grateful for the blessing.

The images flickered across the screens, and the number of viewers increased exponentially, drawn by the simple holo of water released into the sky. No one alive had seen a real geyser before, and the magic of water spraying into the air was like an apparition. The view count quickly climbed into the millions as the holo spread like a virus.

"What have you done?" asked Torq, his voice shrouded with rage.

"We've tapped the aquifer," said Ulysses, "and shown everyone how it's done."

The short holo played again and again. It had been made with the inexpensive security cameras at the dam site and uploaded to the wireless from the simple booth at the gaming center. It carried Will's ID, because he was the one who had uploaded it, and the YouToo! record would soon be set in his name. But I didn't mind, even though it was my idea. Let the world see its fortune: water, billions of liters, still pure and untouched, in hidden aquifers around the globe. Kai would show us, and we would drill, and the rivers would run free once more.

"You're finished," said Ulysses. The bird twitched on his neck. "The world doesn't need you. It doesn't need any of us."

Torq glared at him, but he was powerless. He could kill us, but it would be too late. Kai had given the people water. Where there was water—even just a little—there was hope. And hope was the enemy of despots and tyrants. It shimmered at the edge of the blue stream in the glint of the desert sun.

"It's not over," said Torq. His brown body shook with fury, like a man whose kingdom had burned down around him. "We'll see how long the people remember." Then he turned, heels clicking, and led his men from the room.

It was only then I noticed Sula holding the harpoon behind her back, her hand gripping so tight that her knuckles were white. I touched the woman's arm until her hand relaxed and slipped mine between the warmth and the weapon.

"Come," I said. "Let's go home."

CHAPTER 22

We said good-bye to Kai and Driesen outside the gaming center. In front of everyone, Kai took my hand and kissed me. It was embarrassing but also sweet, even if Will did make a coyote whistle that turned my head at the last minute.

"See you tomorrow?" Kai asked. He was still weak from high blood sugar, but his voice was strong and clear.

Tomorrow was a school day, I realized, an ordinary day, although it seemed like it couldn't be. "I'll see you at the bus stop," I said. I leaned into him, and this time I kissed him back—on the mouth— and I didn't care who was watching.

The black limo was waiting at the corner. Its gasoline engine purred, and the exhaust gathered lazily like a cloud. A new bodyguard held the rear door open, and Kai followed his father inside. For a moment he disappeared behind the darkened and reinforced glass, but as the limo pulled away, he opened the window and waved. The last thing I saw was his blond hair streaming wildly behind him and his mouth open to catch the wind.

Ulysses drove Will and me in his pirates' truck down the dusty road where I had first met Kai. But now I imagined trees shading the shoulders and tall grass swaying in the median. I saw children riding pedicycles and adults walking arm in arm beneath a cool evening sun. I saw the road leading to Basin and beyond, straight and clear and safe. A road that might take us anywhere.

Ulysses parked the truck near the main entrance to our building. He and Sula descended first, and Cheetah bounded out behind them. Will and I stopped by the open gate, taking in the familiar sights of home. Our apartment was just as I remembered it. Painted shutters brightened the windows. Two cacti flowered in a terrarium by the door. A welcome wreath hung from the railing.

We climbed the rickety steps. The lights were off in our neighbor's apartment, although there was nothing unusual about trying to save credits on electricity. I knocked on our door, and the sound echoed hollowly inside.

"Maybe they've gone shopping," said Will dubiously.

We both knew our mother could not leave the house. If our father was gone, something had happened.

I knocked again. This time we heard shuffling and scraping, and then the door opened. Our father stood there, smiling wearily, not surprised at all, as if we had simply returned late from water team.

"We're home," I said.

The man who stepped between us was instantly recognizable. His trim beard and tight face. His white teeth razored perfectly between his lips.

"Hello, Will. Hello, Vera," said the chief administrator.

There was something familiar as well about the two men in

blue shirts who flanked him. Then it came to me: they had been watching Kai at the gaming center. But who were they? And why was the chief administrator here?

"I'm sorry," said our father. "He insisted on waiting for you."

"What's going on, Dad?" asked Will.

Before our father could respond, Cheetah sprang into the room, followed by Ulysses and Sula. One of the blue-shirted men went for his belt, but Sula knocked the gun out of his hand before he could even grip it. Ulysses pulled his gun on the other man while Cheetah held the chief administrator at bay.

"Please!" said the administrator. "There is no need for fisticuffs."

"They just want to talk to you," added our father.

"Then talk," said Ulysses, still holding the gun at the administrator's temple.

"It would be a more pleasant conversation if we could all be seated."

Cheetah growled.

"Talk," repeated Ulysses.

The administrator harrumphed. He was not used to taking orders from pirates, but Cheetah looked as if she was hungry.

"Very well," he said, eyeing the dog. "We understand you've just had an interesting adventure with some of our friends on the coast."

"You know all about it," I said.

"Yes." The administrator tried to smile, but his teeth prevented his lips from closing. "And we know all about your friend as well."

"Kai?"

"Finds water with his nose. Very useful."

"You saw the wi-cast. He can find hidden aquifers."

"How fortunate for the republic. To have this valuable resource right here—in our own town."

"Yes," I said cautiously.

"Not the sort of thing you'd want to waste. By sharing him with another republic, for example."

"That aquifer runs all the way to Minnesota," I said. "And the water that's in it falls from the sky. No one owns it."

"But you're wrong," said the administrator. "The Canadians own it. And the Minnesotans. And the Europeans too." A tiny fleck of blood darkened his lower lip. "Why shouldn't we take what's rightfully ours?"

"Because it's not rightfully ours."

"The boy lives in Illinowa. In Arch. He can make us all wealthy."

"It's that kind of thinking that turned the forests to deserts."

"Don't be naïve, girl. You'll never get the rivers flowing. Your friend Kai needs to help his own people, and we need your help convincing him."

I shook my head. Now I knew why the administrator was here, and why the men had been following Kai at the gaming center. But I would never help him steal the water for himself. I told him none of us would.

"You're making a mistake," he said. "One you will regret."

Ulysses raised his gun, but I silenced him. "No," I said. "It's you who've made the mistake, taking what doesn't belong to you. Now we need you to leave."

"You heard Vera. Leave." Ulysses motioned to the door with his gun, and Sula shoved the man in front of her. Cheetah started barking, and the administrator scampered backward.

"Think about it," he said, as he stumbled out the door. "You won't have another chance."

"Neither will you."

Then I slammed the door behind him.

Our father watched this, wide-eyed and pale. But Will comforted him. "He can't do anything. Otherwise he wouldn't have come here."

"I hope you're right,"

"Kai, Will, and Vera are heroes," said Ulysses reassuringly. "The politicians will think twice before making them enemies."

I told our father then about facing down Torq in the gaming center, and how Ulysses and Sula had saved our lives. Cheetah jumped up and licked our father's face, nearly knocking him over. He was startled at first, but then his face softened. A real dog slobbering before him, protecting his two lost children, brought tears to his eyes. He never imagined he would see such things. Yet here we were. Alive, safe, home.

"You must tell your mother."

He invited everyone inside, but Ulysses and Sula, observing old customs, insisted they would remain outside with the dog. Something flickered between them, ancient and familiar, and it made my heart ache.

"We'll be right back," I promised.

"Don't hurry," said Ulysses. "We're not going anywhere."

Our father led us deeper into the house. It was dark and hushed. Even the wireless was silent. "Rose! Rose!" he called. "You have visitors."

We walked down the hallway and into our mother's room. The shades were drawn, but behind them glowed the suffused light from outdoors—red and gold, the colors of autumn. Will stopped as if he might fling them open. But I pushed him along, and he let it go.

We went to the bedside where our mother slept fitfully. The pillows were scattered behind her like whitecaps on waves. Her face was freckled and pale, and her red hair was pulled back tightly in a bun. A few stray wisps danced at the edges of her mouth.

I touched her arm, and her eyes flickered, then opened. She looked up and smiled as if we had never been gone. "Will. Vera," she said. "I'm so thirsty."

"We brought you some water," I said.

Then I filled a glass and helped her drink.

THE

WATER

WARS

ABOUT THE AUTHOR

© MARION ETTLINGER

Cameron Stracher is the author of *Dinner with Dad* and *Double Billing* and a novel, *The Laws of Return*. He has written for the *New York Times*, the *New York Times Magazine*, and the *Wall Street Journal*, among other publications. When he is not writing, he is a media lawyer who represents newspapers, magazines, and television producers in defamation, privacy, intellectual property, and related matters. A graduate of Amherst College, Harvard Law School, and the Iowa Writers' Workshop, he lives with his wife, two children, and two dogs in Connecticut. Email him at: thewaterwars@gmail.com.